THE SAFEHOUSE

THE CAPTIVE SERIES

DANIELLE BANNISTER

THE SAFEHOUSE

DANIELLE BANNISTER

CITY OWL
PRESS

THE SAFEHOUSE
The Captive, Book 2
By: Danielle Bannister

CITY OWL PRESS
www.cityowlpress.com

Cover Design by MiblArt. All stock photos licensed appropriately.

Edited by Danielle DeVor.

For information on subsidiary rights, please contact the publisher at info@cityowlpress.com.

Print Edition ISBN: 978-1-64898-471-6

Digital Edition ISBN: 978-1-64898-472-3

Printed in the United States of America

ALSO BY DANIELLE BANNISTER

THE ROMANCES

The Sweeter Side

The ABCs of Dee

Doppelganger

Must Love Coffee

Taking Stock

What Moons Do (YA)

Waiting in the Wings

Waiting on the Words

The Sexier Side

The First 100 Kisses

The Second 100 Kisses

Where You Left Me-Vol. 1-5

Arranged Vows Seasons 1 and 2

FANTASY AND PARANORMAL

The Hallowed Realms Trilogy with Amy Miles

The Lurkers Within: A Havenwood Falls Novella

The Twin Flames Trilogy

DARK ROMANCE AND THRILLER

Girl On Fire

The Cage

The Safehouse
The Sanctuary

PRAISE FOR DANIELLE BANNISTER

"Bannister weaved a gripping tale with an original concept making *Pulled* a very enjoyable read. I was never quite sure where the author would direct her characters, what the outcome would be which I really liked. And the final outcome was certainly not what I expected, so bravo!"
— *Two Nerds with Words*

"Reading books from authors that you have read before and you think you know their style of writing, and then BAM!!! They go and write something that is completely off the wall for them, you end up loving that author just a little bit more."
— *Kelly's Nerdy Obsession*

"*The ABC's of Dee* was funny and engaging from the first page. I loved being inside Dee's head as she navigated her hilarious dating adventures. She was honest with herself almost to a fault, but her ongoing inner commentary was refreshing and relatable."
— *Avid Reader*

"*The First 100 Kisses* is Bannister's next standalone. I loved every minute of it! The characters are a great match. Complete opposites. The lessons went from sweet to sinful. It was perfect."
— *Two Book Pushers*

"Holy mac and cheese, or should I say burgers and fries *wink* , *The Second 100 Kisses* is just everything to me right now!! A perfect balance of swoon, smexy, comedy, drama, angst, and character building...all while keeping it real. I devoured these books in one sitting and both left me with all the feels."
— *Book Flirts*

This series is dedicated to the readers who begged for more of this twisted story. See? Good things can come from begging.

AUTHOR'S NOTE

This book is the second in a series. Before you read *The Safehouse*, you need to read *The Cage* or you will be very confused.

RECAP OF THE CAGE

Has it been a minute since you read *The Cage* and can't quite remember what it's about? Here are the rough points to remember.

- Connor runs an illegal 'pet' adoption agency, a.k.a. a human trafficking ring.
- Amanda was tricked into his ring under the promise of a rental unit. A unit she was then locked inside of while Connor prepped her for sale.
- Amanda, using her only weapon against Connor, her feminine prowess, must convince him that he loves her, so he won't sell her off.
- In her bid for survival, the line between who Connor is and who he could be is blurred. Her emotions get jumbled. Does she like Connor or is it just survival instincts?
- Connor, afraid of his own feelings for one of his 'pets,' tries to sell her off to a guy named Malcolm. A guy, ironically, Amanda knew from her childhood, under a different name.

- Malcolm quickly realizes Amanda is not with Connor of her own free will and takes it upon himself to free Amanda by taking her on a trial adoption run.
- Connor finds out that Malcolm has taken his property and goes after him.
- Book one ends with Malcolm and Amanda fleeing, and Connor close on their heels.

CHAPTER ONE

Amanda

For several hours, Malcolm and I didn't speak. We sat in the car as the world passed us by. Each mile marker brought me further away from the cage, but closer to uncertainty. Where were we going? And how long could we outrun a madman?

Then again, maybe I was putting too much weight on Connor's reaction to Malcolm taking me off his hands. Sure, he'd be angry he'd been swindled, but maybe Malcolm was right? Maybe Connor would spend some time searching for us but then give up when it became a burden to his operation. After all, I was one cog in a very big machine. Connor was smart. He wouldn't jeopardize his whole operation for me. He'd be pissed, but when we weren't easily discovered, he'd move on and I would finally be safe.

Everything was in limbo. We didn't know how long we had before Connor discovered Malcolm had taken me. Connor gave him a two-week 'trial run' with me as his pet. So, in theory, we had until then to get to our safe location and hunker down until the dust settled. I was trusting that once we got to Malcolm's safehouse we'd be able to determine if we were being hunted, and more importantly, how to help the women I'd left behind to save myself.

Glancing over at my unwitting knight in shining armor, I saw his eyes drooping. His shoulders were slumped low from hours of driving, yet his hands held the wheel with a death grip.

From the glow of the console, I could make out his strong features. His perfectly squared jaw, a dark beard trimmed close to his skin, and an expensive suit, now wrinkled. His top shirt buttons were undone, and he'd removed his tie a while ago. It was draped against the back seat, the edge of it dangling where I once hid from the threat of being discovered.

Just then, Malcolm let loose a huge yawn.

"Do you want me to drive?" I asked.

"No. We'll stop at the next exit. Grab a hotel. There should be one just past the toll plaza."

"Kinky," I said, then instantly regretted it. "Sorry. Force of habit."

"It's okay. Although, I *am* going to insist we share a room. Not for that," he added quickly. "I don't want you out of my sight until we're at our final destination. If Connor is as cunning as you say he is, I don't want to take any chances."

"So, what, you'll sleep on the floor?" I raised an eyebrow.

He glanced over at me. "I'll get a room with two beds."

"Which the hotel will conveniently be out of," I said. I leaned my head on the glass.

"What?"

I shrugged. "That's how it always happens in books and movies. An attractive couple, who aren't technically a couple, try to check into a hotel with separate rooms or separate beds. But, to the shock of no one, there are no doubles available, and they just *have* to share a bed."

"I'm quite sure the motel will have the accommodations we require."

"Let's bet on it. Loser has to sleep on the floor."

He frowned. "Amanda, I'm not going to let you sleep on the floor."

"You won't need to, because I'm going to win." I stuck out my hand. He sighed, but he took my hand and gave it a small shake.

He didn't let my hand go immediately, and it sent a small shiver through me.

"We'll get off at the next exit. Keep your eyes open."

I looked down at his hand as it slowly pulled away from mine. "They're open."

After the toll, he pulled off at the next exit and, sure enough, there was a hotel. Well, motel. And a crap one at that. The sign was missing two of its letters, and there was an outdoor pool that looked like it hadn't been used in years. A sheen of grime peppered the outside walls. It was a place to sleep for the truly desperate or irrationally horny. Of which I was both.

"Not quite the level of luxury you're used to?" I guessed when he pulled into a spot. Malcolm frowned before he got out of the car. I followed close behind him as he made his way to the trunk to get the bags.

"On the contrary," he said. "This feels like home. Don't forget I grew up dirt poor. But more importantly, it's not where Connor would expect *me* to be, so it's perfect." He closed the trunk and locked the car. "Let's go."

Malcolm was probably right. Connor wouldn't know we'd left the house, let alone the state yet. There was no reason to feel so on edge, and yet, I couldn't help but look over my shoulder as we walked through the parking lot. A yellow school bus took up nearly half of the lot. Great. Rowdy kids and a crap room. Awesome.

Malcolm was about two steps ahead of me. I watched as his eyes darted left to right as though he was scanning for danger. I was right there with him. On edge. With each car I passed, I wondered if Connor might jump out, pull me inside, and speed away before Malcolm could do anything about it. I shook my head, trying to ward off the panic.

Inside, the motel's lobby was little more than the size of a living room. On one wall, a small counter held large plastic containers of assorted generic-looking cereal and a toaster. At least breakfast would be included. Not that Malcolm couldn't afford breakfast elsewhere.

Two small tables for guests to eat at sat near a fake fireplace with a couple of wooden chairs at the window. A small coffee table held heaps of curled-edge magazines. No one was at the front desk.

"Hello?" Malcolm asked the empty room.

I noticed a ding bell on the counter, so I gave it a hard hit.

A moment later, a door opened near the continental breakfast nook. "Oh, hello. I didn't hear ya come in."

An older man with silver hair and a Mr. Roger's style cardigan shuffled behind the counter. His eyes blinked several times as though we'd woken him.

"It's no problem," I offered. "We're sorry to be here so late."

The man waved my apology away before he grabbed a pencil. "Checking in or do you need to book a room?"

"We need one room. Double beds. Paying with cash if that's okay?"

The man nodded and opened up a large paper ledger. There didn't seem to be any sort of computer around. "We only take cash, so you're in luck. We're a bit old school here. Thought it might lose business at first, but there is an ATM around the corner and for the most part, there seems to be a fair amount of people who don't like their whereabouts tracked on those fandangled credit card machines. I don't need Big Brother knowing my business, am I right?" He laughed. His voice was gruff like he smoked a pack a day.

"Privacy is rare these days," Malcolm agreed.

"Indeed, it is. Now, let's see what we have. Just got in a bus full of basketball kids, so they've cleaned me out pretty good. But I think I might have..." He flipped a few pages. Then flipped back one. "Well, looks like the best I can offer you is a single with a king bed. Seventy-five dollars a night. Free breakfast and coffee from five to ten a.m. That work for ya?"

I looked up at Malcolm and smiled, whispering, "'I told you so" to him.

Malcolm frowned. "Are the floors carpeted?"

"They are."

"We'll take it." He slid a hundred-dollar bill at the man. "You can keep the change."

The man's eyes lit up. "Well, thank you, sir. And a name?"

"Jack—"

"Gavin. Mr. and Mrs. Gavin. We just got married. She's still not used to my name," Malcolm said. He pulled me to him and kissed the top of my head. I realized my blunder immediately.

"Damn," I said. "I need to remember that, huh?" I slid my arm around him too and stood on my tiptoes to plant a kiss on him. He froze at first but then relented and allowed the moment to happen. *Fuck.* He was a great kisser.

I only pulled away when the man at the desk cleared his throat. Malcolm held onto my bottom lip with his teeth for a second before he finally let me go.

"Sorry. Newlyweds." I blushed.

"You two enjoy your stay now," he said. I noticed he glanced down at my left hand. No wedding band on it. "Here's your key. First floor, about three doors down from here." He glanced between us one last time before he shuffled back off to his room.

With the large gold key on an oversized plastic keychain spouting the hotel's name, I took one of the bags off the floor and tossed it over my shoulder. It weighed significantly more than I was prepared for.

"Jesus, what do you have in here, a dead body?" I asked.

Malcolm grabbed the bag from off my shoulder and easily put it over his, picking the other off the ground as well. "I like to be prepared for anything. Sue me."

"Pfft. Like I could afford to sue anyone. I don't have a dime on me," I said.

He paused in the doorway, our bodies nearly touching. "Then you best not leave my side, Mrs. Gavin."

I knew what he was saying. Don't be stupid. Don't try to run or be self-sacrificing.

"Would you spank me if I did, *Mr. Gavin?*" I couldn't help the flirtatious tone that escaped my lips. Malcolm didn't miss it either as he inhaled deeply. I'd made him uncomfortable. Good. Standing tall, I held up my left hand. "If we're gonna keep up this married act, I'm gonna need a ring. A big one." I winked.

"Right. We should come up with a story. Let's get some rest for now. Long day tomorrow."

I bowed my head and let him pass. I couldn't help but admire the view. The man had an impressive build. I had to give him that. And he was strong. Those bags were not light. It made me curious about what the hell was in there. And how unfazed I'd be if it *did* turn out to be a dead body. Nothing was going to surprise me anymore. Except maybe what spending the night in the same room with Malcolm would be like.

MALCOLM

The hotel room was just as horrific as I imagined it would be. The walls were covered in floor-to-ceiling fake wood paneling, on which hung several attempts at art. The lighting was a lovely flickering fluorescent, while the floors looked like puke. The yellow and brown shag rug in front of the door was threadbare at the entrance and likely hadn't seen a vacuum in months.

"Yeah, you're not sleeping on that carpet," Amanda said.

She was sitting on the "king" bed that was a queen at best.

"There's plenty of room here. And I don't bite. Well, I do, but I'll try and keep my hands to myself." She flashed her perfect smile at me, but I looked away.

Her flirtation was not directed at me. It was her default setting around men. "Amanda, you don't need to do that, you know." I placed the bags on the bed beside her.

"I'm not letting you sleep on that carpet—"

"No. Not that. The sexual innuendos. You don't have to do that with me. You don't need to flirt with me to ensure your safety. I'm not going to hurt you."

I studied her face as she took in my words. She obviously wasn't used to someone treating her with respect. Given her past relationship with men, it wasn't hard to understand why. She needed to know, however, that I wasn't like them. And the only way to convey that was to keep my hands off her. No matter how much I might want to push her down on that bed and— *No. Malcolm. She's not an object. You're here to help her. Nothing more.*

"I'm sorry," Amanda said. "Force of habit. I guess I'm just used to men wanting something from me."

"The only thing I want is for you to be as far away from Connor Brooks as we can get you."

She studied me for a moment as though she was deciding if I could be trusted or not. Gnawing on her lip, she cocked her head. "And once I'm safe, then we'll talk about how to save the other women?"

I nodded. "Yes. I promise. I'll find a way to free them too. But only once I have you safe. Deal?" I held out my hand to shake hers.

She looked at my outstretched hand almost as though she were debating with herself if she could take me at my word.

"Amanda, I know believing I won't hurt you is a tall order. Not only am I virtually a stranger, but I'm a man. And I know in your life men have not been all that reliable. All I'm asking is for two days to get you to my safehouse."

"And then you'll ask me for sex?" Amanda smirked.

I frowned at her.

"I was kidding, calm down." She laughed, but with an edge to it. "Seeing as how I don't have a ton of other options." She held out her hand for me to shake.

Our hands met as we shook, and I tried hard to ignore the shiver that went down my spine from her touch. She ran her thumb inside the palm of my hand.

"You have big hands."

"I do."

"You know what that means, don't you?" She smiled as her eyes darted unmistakably to my crotch.

"No. What does it mean?" I challenged.

"Big hands, large...gloves." She pulled her hand away and backed herself over to the bed, grinning the whole time. She had never been more beautiful.

"So, what's really in these bags?" She tapped one of them with her foot.

"See for yourself." I walked over to her and unzipped the bag she'd kicked, so she could see inside. Her eyes nearly fell out of her head.

"Holy shit!" She dropped to her knees and pulled free two large wads of money. "Is this all filled with money?"

"And passports, foreign currency, legal documents, burner phones...that sort of thing."

"And what's in the other one? Gold bricks?" she shrieked.

"Nothing quite so grand. Clothing, hair dye, scissors, protein bars, medicine, and a first aid kit. Basic vanishing essentials."

"Jesus, you *are* prepared. Do you use these often?"

I sighed and sat on the edge of the bed. "I use them frequently enough to know what to put in a go-bag."

"A 'go-bag.'" She snickered, then stood up. "That's oddly hot." At that, she flinched. "Sorry. Jesus, I can't stop flirting with you."

I wanted to comfort her but that wasn't my place. Instead, I offered her the next best thing. "Why don't you grab the shower first? I'm going to map our route for tomorrow. I want to throw in some side roads to make sure we aren't being followed. Might take us a little longer, but we've got nothing but time."

"You don't have to ask me twice. A hot shower sounds amazing. With actual soap to boot."

"He didn't give you soap?" I seethed.

"He barely let us shower. Unless he was the one doing the bathing. He doesn't trust us with anything that isn't bolted down. Literally. There is nothing in those cages that could be used to hurt him or ourselves."

My hands balled into fists. "Did he hurt you? Physically?"

Amanda gnawed at the bottom of her lip. "Nothing I couldn't handle. But the other girls...they got it worse. Especially if I didn't listen to him."

"Why would it be worse for them if you didn't listen?" I was thoroughly confused. She shrugged.

"Because instead of hurting me for not obeying, he'd beat them. Fastest way to make us comply. Connor knew we'd be sympathetic. Which is why we need to make sure to save them. When he discovers you stole me... He'll take it out on them."

My blood was boiling, imagining the hell she must have endured. The favors she must have granted to protect herself or the others. "I'll find a way to make him pay for everything he's done to you."

She ran her fingers up her arm as though holding herself. "Yeah, well now you know why I was willing to go back to him. If I could save even one of them..."

"Even if it meant risking your own life?"

"Absolutely," she said without hesitation. "I'm expendable. No one would miss me if I were gone."

"I would," I said. I was surprised by how honest that answer was. "Which is why you can't go back now. I'd miss you too much." I walked over to her and placed a hand on her shoulder. She flinched slightly. "Promise me, Amanda. Promise you won't try to go back there. I'll find a way to save those girls, but I refuse to sacrifice you to do it. I need you to trust me."

"Trust?" She raised her eyebrows. "No offense, but that's the word every man who has ever hurt me has used."

Her words gutted me in a way I wasn't prepared for. While I knew she held no shred of deception when she confessed that, however, convincing her I wasn't like them would be one of the hardest things I'd ever have to do.

"You're right," I said. "I'm sorry. I can't ask you to trust me. That needs to be earned. So that's what I'm going to do, Amanda.

From this moment on. I'm going to do whatever I can to earn your trust. However long that takes. Okay?"

Her eyes met mine for a moment, and I swear tears were there, but she gave me a nod before heading into the bathroom to take her shower.

Satisfied she wasn't going to try to escape through the bathroom window, I took that time to go through the bags. Snatching the first one from off the floor, I tossed it onto the bed and pulled out a few paper maps. I didn't trust using the car's GPS. I wasn't sure how sophisticated Connor's tracking skills were. Travel was a big part of my job, so reading maps and road signs was not unfamiliar to me.

I wasn't looking for the fastest route, I was searching for the off-the-beaten paths Connor, or his men, might not think to look.

From my suit jacket pocket, I tugged free a small notepad. I flipped open the metal casing around it that had my initials engraved in it. My real initials. DL. I ran the pad of my thumb over the cursive. My mom gave it to me on my seventeenth birthday. She was a bit of a note-taker herself, always jotting things down. She passed that trait onto me. I'd used this same notepad holder ever since. Every time I'd take it out, I would think of her and how happy she'd been to give me such a fancy gift. Money was always tight, but she'd found the case at a thrift store and paid to have it engraved.

Looking at the map, there were two choices. After we got off I-90 we'd either take I-94 or I-82. The latter would take about an hour longer.

In the notebook, I jotted down: I-90 E, I-82 E, I-84 E, I-80 E, then hop onto I-90 E.

Closing the pad, I slipped it back into my jacket and refolded the map, tossing it back in the bag. The map landed on one of the burner phones. I debated calling to check in but that wasn't protocol. Twenty-four hours. Minimum. Darcy and Camila needed time to align their alibis. Not to mention their hands would be full closing up the house. So far so good. Even with the extra travel time, everything should be buttoned up within a few days. So far so good.

CHAPTER TWO

Connor

Kenny met me at the abandoned dry cleaners. Of all the men that I've employed over the years, Kenny has been with me the longest. Does that mean I trusted him? Hell no. I don't trust anyone. But if I wanted anyone in the crew as a second pair of eyes, it was Kenny. He was a hunter. And he had no issues with brutality. Two things I needed to track down Malcolm.

The sun had set, so the cover of night shielded our entrance into the building. We could have had this conversation on the phone, but I wanted to make sure we weren't being traced. I had no idea what Malcolm's people might have on their end for hackers. I highly doubted they were as good as mine, but I had to be careful.

"Who's the target?" Kenny asked once we were both inside.

"Amanda Jackson."

Kenny raised an eyebrow. "Your new foster? She ran?"

"No. She was stolen. By Malcolm Luxx. I gave him a trial run with her, and the second I left, he packed her up and skipped town."

"Well, that was stupid," Kenny said. He fingered the gun holstered at his hip.

Nodding, I ran my hands through my hair. There was a knot in my stomach that almost felt like worry. And I never got worried. "Very stupid. Nobody steals from me."

"So, what's the play? Take them down? Or bring them back for torture?"

"Torture is a thought. I would love nothing more than to give Malcolm a slow and drawn-out death, but an offense like theft demands that he die. Preferably by my hand. If you find him, notify me before you take a shot. If I can get to him to deal with him myself, without the window closing, I want to be the one to do it. If not, you have your orders."

Kenny nodded. "And the girl."

I locked eyes with him. "She lives. I don't want a single hair on her body harmed. Until I know what went down. I need to know if she's compromised our setup. Understood?"

"The girl comes back with me. Got it." He nodded and turned to leave; his orders given. I grabbed his shirt.

"Kenny, your dick stays in your pants. You and your hunters don't get to pillage this one."

Kenny looked at me, clearly taken aback. "But—"

"I know that's our normal terms. I'll pay you double."

"I don't understand. Why would you care if—"

I yanked him so that we were nose to nose. "She's *mine*." Kenny's eyes grew wide. I'd let my mask slip. He couldn't know I cared about her.

I let him go and tried to regain my composure. "She's, my responsibility. If she ran from me, I'll make her wish she were dead, and when I'm through with her punishment, then you can have what's left of her. But if Malcolm stole her, I have to know what she knows. I need to hear it from her lips. Are we clear?"

He nodded slowly. "You got it. But you'll be paying triple my normal fee. Not double. The men will need a damn good reason not to get their dicks wet with that one."

I let him go and nodded. I would have paid him quadruple.

Kenny left then. He'd gather his best hunters. The job would be done within a few hours. They'd never taken longer than ten hours to clean up a runaway. This one might prove harder, however. The escapee had a helper. A rich one. A recluse used to hiding in plain sight. I worried this hunt might be more than Kenny's team could handle.

In the meantime, I needed to do some digging of my own. I knew just where to start. And that lead was all thanks to Amanda.

Back at my place, I booted up my computer and pulled up Malcolm's file. More specifically, the one piece of information Malcolm didn't know that I had. His real name. Not a lot of Dayton Littlefields in Waldo, Maine. There were only two, in fact, at the time he lived there. And one was a man in his eighties. A bit more searching on the web gave me the younger Littlefield's old mailing address. After a few calls and a few favors, I tracked him to New Hampshire. A few years after that move, Dayton Littlefield was mentioned in the death notice of his mother. Here's the curious part, a woman by his dead mother's *exact* name buys a cottage just two years ago in the middle woods in Bum-Fuck Nowhere, New Hampshire. A quaint little spot for a safehouse.

"Gotcha."

I whipped out my cell phone and called Kenny. "Where are you right now?"

"I've got a crew combing Seattle, and I'm checking all the bus stations—"

"Bring them all in. I know where she is." I looked at the property on the real estate's website with the proud SOLD sign advertising the address of the cabin. "Or where she's going to be in the next few days."

"Where?"

"I'll send you the address on the burner. Gas up the SUVs, boys. We're going on a road trip."

I hung up the phone and glared at the screen showing Malcolm's smug smile.

"I fucking got you, Malcolm. I fucking got you. If you've laid one finger on Amanda..."

I shoved out of my chair and texted Kenny the address and

told him where to meet me. I had to pack my bags quickly. Kenny would see that we had enough in terms of weapons, but I brought my stash too. I needed to be ready.

Slinging the bags over my shoulder, I made a call I was dreading.

"Dad. It's Connor. Look, I'm going to pick you up in about an hour. I need you to come and stay at my place for a few days. Something is going down, and I can't have you out there as leverage to use against me."

"Law after you again?" My dad laughed in his sloppy-drunk way.

"Something like that. Look, just pack up your bottles and be ready when I pull up. It should only be for a few days."

"I've never been to your place before." He hiccupped. "I don't know how to get there."

I pinched my hand over the bridge of my nose. "I know, Dad. And you don't need to know how to get here. I'm driving you."

"But I like my place, Connie."

I wanted to reach through the phone and strangle him. "If you're not ready when I get there, I'll never pay another bookie of yours, ever. Understood?"

That shut him up. "I'll be ready."

I hung up and let loose a breath. I didn't think Malcolm would be cruel enough to use my father against me, but if I were him, I'd use any and all assets at my disposal. Better to take this one off the menu.

One last call to make, then I could take back what was mine.

"Anita, I know it's not your day to clean, but if you want to make a quick five grand, I have a job for you." I smiled as I heard her broken English process what I'd asked. She complied quickly. "Perfect. Yeah, I need you to come and feed the pets while I'm gone for a few days. *Bueno. Sí, Sí.* I'll leave the food in Stacey's refrigerator, the unit that was just cleaned. Anita, this is important. My father will be staying at my place for a few days. He will be caged inside until I return. He is not to be let out or spoken to. Understood? Excellent. You get half wired to you now and half upon my return."

Was it risky leaving the pets under her supervision? Absolutely. I normally wouldn't leave the feeding and training of my pets to anyone but me, but I couldn't exactly let Kenny have all the fun. Not when I knew where they would fucking be.

It wasn't like Anita was an unknown either. She'd worked with me since the very beginning. She knew what went on here. She knew my work paid her and kept her in this country. She wouldn't be stupid enough to risk her livelihood. Living in danger of immigration made even the best people do despicable things. Not to mention, I had cameras everywhere. If she tried anything, I'd know it.

My father was the only real loose cannon in this situation. Not that I owed my father a damn thing after how absent he'd been growing up. If anything, I protected his ass because it's what Mother would expect of me. I honestly didn't care if he drank himself into an early grave. It would certainly save me some money.

But because he still walked the earth, he was a liability. Someone that could be used as leverage. And I wasn't about to allow that. So I'd collect him, hide him, and then release him when Amanda was back.

The hiding him part would be annoying. He didn't technically know *how* I made my money. Nor did he care so long as I bailed him out whenever his gambling debt got too high. Now I would be forced to let him into my world. I'd need to lock him in my apartment, of course, but that was something I could handle easily enough. Getting people inside a cage was as easy as breathing. It was only when they tried to get out that they realized they weren't in Kansas anymore. Maybe I'd be in luck, and he'd get so drunk he'd pass out cold the whole time. That way I could spin some lie about why I had to lock him in. It didn't matter right now. The only thing that mattered was getting my property back.

And putting a bullet in between Malcolm's eyes.

AMANDA

The hot water against my skin was like a balm to my aching bones. The hotel didn't have the same fancy soaps and lotions that Malcolm's shower had, but it was better than what I had in the cage, which was nothing.

As I lathered the thin generic soap, I noted that the red welt on my ass from where Connor had hit me was finally gone, but not the hickey he'd left on my inner thigh. I scrubbed at it harder, willing those conflicting memories to wash themselves from my mind.

Had what Malcolm said about Stockholm Syndrome been right? Had my desire for Connor been a defense mechanism? I'd never been turned on quite like that when I was with Sam or other boyfriends, but then again, I wasn't in the same level of danger with them. Sure, my life was always potentially on the line, but even in those awful situations, I could leave. I rarely did, but the door to my bad choices wasn't locked as it had been with Connor. Was the desire I felt my body's way of keeping me alive? Or was I just a twisted fuck? My money was on the latter.

The water-thin shampoo did little to hydrate my hair and the conditioner was laughable at best. I would be one ball of frizz once it all dried. Still, it was an improvement.

When I got out of the shower, a box of black hair dye and a pair of rubber gloves laid on the sink. I hadn't even heard Malcolm come in to drop them off. Grabbing a towel, I couldn't help but wonder if he'd snuck a peek at me through the glass doors. If the roles had been reversed, I would have.

Wrapping the towel around me, I grabbed the box and went into the room. Malcolm was looking in a mirror, shaving off his beard.

"Black?" I asked.

"I figured that would be easier than blonde, but I have that too if you'd rather." He looked up at me then from his shaving, noticing I was just in a towel. His eyes widened as he quickly processed what he was seeing before he went back to the mirror, flushed.

"No, black is better. It's just going to be a bitch to get back to my natural color when this is all over."

"I'm sorry, Amanda. I wish this wasn't necessary."

I nodded. "Me too. But you're right. Though you should probably trim your hair, too. The clean face isn't much of a shift." It would be a pity to lose those waves, but desperate times...

He held up the scissors. "That's up next. You any good at haircutting? If not, I'll buzz it."

"God, don't buzz it. Then there would be nothing to grab onto."

He looked at me through the mirror. "Grab onto?"

I blushed. "You know. During sex. Women like something to hang onto."

His lips twitched. "Yes, well, seeing as how sex isn't on my agenda, that hardly matters."

I let free a breath. "Let me start the dye, then I'll come back and give you a trim. Keeping some length in the back." I winked.

I wasn't a stranger to hair dye. I used to have a boyfriend who liked my hair a lighter shade of red than my natural color. At least I didn't have to use bleach. That smell was the worst. Black, however, was a first. I'm not sure I'd recognize myself with black hair. Which, I supposed, was the whole point. Connor and his goons, if they came looking, would be searching for a redhead and a billionaire. The more drastic the change in our looks, the better.

I did my best not to destroy the sink with the dye or have it drip down my face. There wasn't any Vaseline, so I ran some wet soap around my forehead and hoped for the best. The gloves in the kit were all but useless, but I did what I could. When I was done, I washed my hands and cleaned up the sink, tossing the box into the trash.

"Now we wait," I said to my reflection.

Back in the room, Malcolm was finished with his shave. He was sitting on the bed with a change of clothes.

"I'm going to hop in the shower so my hair is wet for your cut."

"Good thinking," I said.

"There are some protein bars in the bag if you're hungry. We'll stop at a convenience store tomorrow and grab some more provisions."

I nodded. "Can't have a road trip without snacks."

Malcolm gave me a small smile. "Back in a sec."

Plopping on the bed, I sighed. Oddly content despite the circumstances. I started the day thinking I was going to be sold off to some sexual pervert and instead, I was being rescued like I was some damsel in distress. Which, I hate to admit, I was. But was Malcolm the Knight in Shining Armor he seemed to be or was he yet another man who would take advantage of the situation of our forced proximity? Lure me into a false sense of security, then take advantage?

Only time would tell with that one. In the meantime, I'd need to keep my guard up. My heart, as shattered and held together with duct tape as it was, needed defending.

Lying on the bed, I propped my wrapped-up hair on the headboard, watching the minutes tick by. After fifteen minutes, Malcolm was still in the shower. I needed to rinse this off before it seeped into my brain.

I got up to check how much longer he'd be, but when I got to the door, I noticed it was slightly ajar. I heard a noise that didn't sound like a shower. But more like... *No. It couldn't be.* I pushed the door open a little more to see what was going on and...OMG. He was jacking off.

Standing there in my towel, gaping at him through the glass door as he worked himself into a frenzy, I found myself wildly turned on. While I couldn't see every detail of his beautiful body thanks to the steam, there was no mistaking what he was doing, or why he'd been taking so long in the shower.

Fuck me, why was this so hot?

Just then, he let out a stifled moan as his hand slammed against the shower door. It nearly pushed it off its track. The sounds of his recovering panting indicated to me that he'd just come.

Smirking, I dropped my towel and got into the shower with him.

"Amanda! What are you—"

"Calm down. I've seen your cock already, remember? And you've already seen my tits. I need to rinse this off and you were taking forever. Now help me rinse it out."

I positioned myself under the showerhead as he bumbled around, trying to cover himself while also diverting his eyes.

"Malcolm, seriously. It's just a naked body. And you've already come, so you're no threat to me. Just help me get this out of my hair, please."

"You saw me?"

My lips curled into a smile. "I sure did. You have great form. Now rinse me."

While I could tell he was mortified, he followed my instructions and began to run his fingers through my newly dyed hair. This rescue mission might not be so bad after all.

CHAPTER THREE

Malcolm

This was a dangerous game we were playing. I knew she was behaving like this as a test. She wanted to see what I'd do with her this close to me and naked. Would I be like every other man in her life and try to possess her body, or would I be trustworthy and help her rinse her hair as asked?

It took all my willpower to put my hands into her hair instead of on her hips and draw her to me. Thankfully, I had just jacked off, so my dick was far more cooperative. I still couldn't believe she'd watched me do that. Or that I hadn't even noticed her eyes on me. Or maybe, subconsciously, I had and that's why I came so hard.

Either way, the only thing I could allow myself to focus on was washing the dye from her hair. I needed to ignore the black streaks that ran down her back and over her perfectly lush ass. *Malcolm. Focus.*

Shaking my head, I forced my eyes back to her head and worked my fingertips into her scalp, massaging the color from her hair. She let slip a soft moan as I worked her scalp, and I had to bite my tongue.

"That feels really good," she purred. "You have magical fingers."

She looked up at me with a wicked grin, knowing full well what she was doing. I couldn't fall for the bait. I had to stay strong.

"My hands get a lot of use as a painter. Okay, you should be good back here. The water is running clear."

She looked down at her hair and nodded before she turned around to rinse a final time. Her perfect breasts on full display now tempting me to reach out and—

"I'll get you a towel," I said. I got out of the shower before I did something stupid.

I picked up my towel and wrapped it around my waist. Then, I set out the last clean towel for her, and promptly left the bathroom. This woman was pushing my boundaries, and I couldn't give in. I refused to be like the other men in her life. Despite how turned on she made me.

As quickly as I could, I dried myself off and put on clothes for the night. I laid out a set of sweats and a T-shirt for her. Camila, in her rush to get clothes together for us, either forgot or intentionally left out any undergarments for Amanda. My bet was on the former. Something I'd have to remedy. We couldn't both be commando. The more layers between our bodies the better.

I moved the go-bags to the center of the bed, creating a physical barrier between the two sections of the bed. It might be overkill but I would need the constant reminder to keep my hands at bay.

Sitting on the far side of the bed, I waited until she came out of the shower. Her newly jet-black hair against her alabaster skin made her look like a modern-day Snow White. While I preferred her natural color, the black awoke something in me as well.

"I look like a Goth Girl." She frowned.

"You're stunning," I said. Her eyes lit up, and I realized that was probably inappropriate. "And it's only temporary. We can get it back to your original color soon."

"Right." She looked at the clothes on the bed.

"These for me?"

I nodded. "Sorry there isn't any underwear. It looks like they didn't pack any in the rush to leave. I'd offer you some of mine, but—"

"You don't wear them."

"How did you—" She raised an eyebrow. Right. She noticed in the car when she tried to blow me.

"It's fine." She dropped her towel then, and I quickly diverted my eyes. Probably not fast enough though.

"What's with the bags on the bed?" She pulled on her clothing.

"I thought maybe you'd appreciate the barrier."

She surprised me by pushing the bags off the bed. "I'm not a kid. I can share a bed with a man."

I risked a look at her. Once I confirmed she was dressed, I stood up and grabbed the scissors.

"Fair enough. Your turn to make me beautiful," I said, holding up the blades. She clapped her hands and came over to me, snatching them from my hands.

"Come sit on the toilet so we don't get hair on the carpet," she said. She held out her hand to me.

Unsure, I took her hand, and she yanked me back to the bathroom, which was still steamy from our shower. She plopped me down on the toilet so that I was straddling it and facing the tank.

"Okay, I'm thinking we can thin the sides here but this spot," she reached her fingers into my hair and gave the back portion of it a gentle but firm tug, "this stays long. Gah, that's the perfect length for latching onto," she said appreciatively.

"I'll take your word on that."

"Oh, come on. You've never had a woman grab your hair there during wild sex?"

"Not that I recall."

"Then you haven't had wild sex." She laughed.

"No. Probably not." I flinched, realizing I shouldn't have revealed that nugget of truth.

She ran her fingers through the side of my hair, tugging gently at it a few times before she made her first cut. I suppressed a moan of my own. She was right, someone touching your hair did feel surprisingly good.

"Hair pulling is very erotic," she said definitively. "If it's done right. A lot of guys will just yank the hair from the ends. That's not sexy. That just hurts. It's when they dig their fingers in, right at the root, and just hold on, locking you in place so that they can properly ravage you. *That's* hot." She sighed. "I don't know, that just gets me, I guess. That feeling of someone not wanting to let me go." She stopped cutting. "Wow. I just heard myself. Abandonment issues, much? Damn."

"I think all people struggle with that," I said. "The feeling of not wanting to be alone. To have someone there with you. Even if they aren't right for you. At least they are there."

She was quiet for a moment before she started cutting again. "Who was that for you?" she asked. "The person you tolerated being in your life, but you knew wasn't right?"

"Every woman I've ever dated." I let loose a small laugh. "I don't know. Maybe it's me. Maybe I'm not meant to be with someone. I'm not the easiest person to get along with."

"Same," she whispered.

For the next several minutes she cut my hair, only asking me to tilt my head or shift back. No further discussion of our failed love lives, which was probably for the best.

"There," she said when she was finished. She spun me around so I was facing her as she examined her work. She stood right in front of me and ran her fingers through my hair, tugging at the strands in the back. "Perfect." She smiled.

I looked up at her. Her hands were still in my hair. Her body was dangerously close to me. It would be far too easy to reach up, take her by the wrists, push her against the wall, and— I stood up then, causing her to take a shaky step backward.

"We should get some sleep. I want to get an early start."

Her eyes were watching me closely, as though she could read my mind about what I really wanted to do to her. I had to keep my wits. Think with my head and not my cock. She was counting on me to keep her safe. Annoyed with myself for wanting to take her in my arms, I did the opposite and pushed past her and went over to the bed. Plopping down on it, I felt my shoulders slump. A moment later, Amanda perched herself lightly on the bed.

"I did it again, didn't I?" Her voice sounded small. Far away.

Glancing over my shoulder, I watched her get into the bed and pull the covers up to her chin.

"Did what?" I asked.

"Was overtly sexual with you." It was her turn to frown. "I wish I knew why I did that. Why I have such a twisted need to make men want to fuck me. It's not like I'm a sex addict or anything. Most of the time, I don't even like sex... So why am I always so flirtatious?" She sounded genuinely angry with herself.

Pulling back the sheets, I got into the bed with her and turned off the lamp, plunging us into darkness. The only light that came in was from the thin crack of light from the parking lot spilling in through the partially closed curtains.

"I'm not a psychiatrist," I said. "Nor do I know what it's like to be a woman, but if I had to take a guess, the reason you're flirtatious has more to do with protection than it does desire."

She spun to her side to look at me through the dark.

"How do you mean?"

"Well," I began, "it sounds like from a very young age you've had to deal with men wanting to take control of your body and mind. You can either choose to ignore the advances, in which case, these disgusting examples of men will just take what they want by force, or you can give them what they want but under your terms. That way you regain some power, some control in what your brain is telling you is the worst of the two evils."

I tried to watch her eyes in the dark, but they were impossible to make out clearly. I wasn't sure if I'd just crossed a line by blurting an opinion that wasn't asked for or if I'd hit the nail on the head.

"I'm sorry if that came out insensitive."

"No. No. You're right. That's exactly what I was doing. I guess

I never realized that was the reason behind it. Give them what they wanted before they hurt me to take it. Damn. That's fucked up."

"No more fucked up than what I do."

"Which is?" Her voice peaked with curiosity.

"I avoid people. Well, women. Unless they are lesbians and want nothing to do with me. Like my assistants. I don't know how to behave around them. I don't want to risk acting like a fool, so I purposefully don't choose to be in the same room with them."

"So sharing a bed right now with a woman must be torture for you?"

"It's not without its challenges."

"Do I make you that uncomfortable?" she asked.

I debated on whether or not I should tell her the truth. "Surprisingly, I'm okay around you. Until you get too close. Then my brain scrambles a bit."

I heard her giggle. It made me smile.

"Is this distance okay? How close we are right now? In the bed? I just want to make sure I'm giving you enough space."

"This is okay, yes," I admitted. I hated how much my voice gave away the smile that had spread across my face.

She surprised me by scooting closer to me. "How about now?"

I tensed up as she approached. "Amanda," I cautioned.

"Too close?" she whispered.

I didn't say anything. I couldn't. My heart was beating too fast. I didn't understand what she was doing, but I also didn't want her to stop.

"How about this?" She tucked herself against my body. "Are you uncomfortable when I am this close?"

"No, I'm not uncomfortable, but I'm not—"

"I know," she whispered. "You're not going to have sex with me. Which is the only reason I'm so close to you. I'm seeing what it feels like to be held by a man who doesn't want anything from me in return." I felt her head lift off from where she had rested it on my shoulder to look at me. "Would you be comfortable with that?"

"You want me to hold you?" I clarified.

"If that's okay?"

There was something quite vulnerable in her tone. She was scared to ask for something she wanted. She didn't want to have sex with me either. She just wanted someone to hold her. Given all that she'd been through the last few days, it was no wonder she was craving such an embrace. She wanted to feel safe. Protected. And I would be an asshole to refuse her.

To answer her, I wrapped my arms around her until she settled her head on my chest. We didn't say anything else. We just lay there, each holding onto the other, listening to the sound of our breathing, until we both ended up falling asleep, still deep in the embrace.

CONNOR

"Almost there, Dad." I grabbed his elbow in the elevator to steady him from dropping to the ground. I didn't bother with the blindfold getting him into the building, as he seemed drunk enough not to remember where he'd been. Besides, I didn't have enough time to cover a blindfolded person being forced inside my place of business. I was in a rush. The sooner he was secured, the faster I could start my hunt for Amanda.

Patricia stood up from her spot at the front desk as we entered, clearly surprised I had someone with me. She didn't know what my father looked like, nor was I about to tell her now. The less people knew about him, the better.

"Tell no one you saw this man," I'd instructed her. She nodded and sat back down at her desk, eyes glued to the ground, as instructed.

Now that we were almost to my unit, the reality of locking him in my place gave me pause. What if he got lucid enough to somehow unlock my computer or snoop around and find something? I couldn't risk it.

The elevator doors opened, and I shuffled him down the hall to Amanda's cage. He could hang out there until I got back. I'd make sure Anita gave him a bottle, and that would take care of everything.

"Here you go, Dad. My apartment is right here." I waited for the scan to finish running across my eyes before I opened the door and helped him to the couch. He plopped down willingly.

"Oh, fancy couch," Dad said. He ran his thick fingers over the edge. "Not one for decoratin',' are ya?" he asked, gesturing around the bare walls. "Not that I know much about anything. Old drunk that I am."

I looked down at my dad in his wrinkled suit that he probably hadn't changed out of in days. His thin gray hair was overdue for a cut, and there was a grease stain on his tie. Mother would be disgusted with how far he'd fallen.

"You know what, Dad? You're right. You are an old drunk. That ends today. This is your intervention. You'll be staying in this room until you dry up. Someone will see you get food."

I didn't wait for him to answer. I just closed the door behind me and locked him in. I should have done this years ago. If he wouldn't sober up on his own, I'd make him. I'd treat him like one of my pets and mold him into the person I wanted him to be.

"Connor," he called after me. "Connie, that's not funny. Open the door." He began pounding on the door. All the pounding in the world wouldn't get him out of the cage now.

Ignoring his pleas, I set about the task of prepping a week's worth of food for the pets and the plus one. I doubted I'd be gone that long, but I wanted to play it safe.

Once the fridge was stocked and instructions for Anita were left, I went back to my unit, grabbed my stuff, and headed for my car.

Let the hunt begin.

CHAPTER FOUR

Amanda

I woke up tucked deep inside Malcolm's arms. The weight of him pressed against me, locking me beside him, was shocking. Unfamiliar and not at all unpleasant.

Cracking an eyelid, I saw that the sun was just starting to tinge the black sky a light blue. It must be around four if I had to guess. It was no surprise that Malcolm was still asleep. His chest rose and fell slowly and rhythmically, lulling me to forget my fears and revel in this moment of calm.

"You okay?" his gruff morning voice asked. It startled me.

"Yeah. I'm good. What time is it?"

He shifted his left arm to check his watch, his right still holding me beside him. "Three forty-seven. You should sleep a few more hours."

"Hmm. But first, I need to pee," I confessed. It was only then that he released me. The skin his arm had been holding now felt the chill of the air without him there.

"I'm going to check in with my team, but we should plan to hit the road no later than seven."

I nodded and headed for the bathroom while he went to grab a burner phone.

After using the bathroom, I washed my hands and swished my

mouth with the small bottle of mouthwash left on the hotel toiletry tray to get rid of my morning breath. I'd need to get a toothbrush when we stopped for provisions. Squinting into the mirror, I flinched a little at my reflection. I wasn't used to the black yet. It made me look paler than I already was.

I splashed some cold water on my face, then headed back to the bed, when I stopped short. Malcolm was frantically getting his clothes on and shoving his belongings in one of the go-bags.

"What's wrong?" I asked. The hairs on my neck started to rise.

"He knows."

"What?"

"Connor. He knows we're gone. We need to leave. Now. Get dressed. I'll check us out and grab us some breakfast. We won't be able to stop for a bit. We need to get some miles between us."

I stood there frozen as Malcolm dug free a change of clothes for me and tossed them on the bed. He whizzed by me to get his things from the bathroom.

Nausea bubbled in the pit of my stomach as the room began to spin. *He knows.* He knows I ran, or worse, that Malcolm took me away from him. That meant Malcolm's life was very much in danger.

"Amanda," Malcolm said. He was suddenly standing in front of me. When I didn't budge, he grabbed both of my arms and gave them a slight shake. "Amanda, did you hear me? We have to go. You know what, you can get dressed in the car. We got to move." He shoved the clothes into my hands before he grabbed both bags.

Blinking a few times, I felt my feet moving out of the room as I followed Malcolm to the car. He put me in the back seat again and buckled me in because my limbs didn't seem to be working. He tossed the clothes beside me.

"Stay here. I'll be two minutes."

He shut the door and locked the Tahoe behind him.

How long had we been asleep? Six hours? Seven? If Connor had found out yesterday, he could be right on our tails. They could be anywhere by now. Which meant Malcolm was not safe. And it was my fault.

Unless I took action. I could get out of the car right now...find some way to get in touch with Connor. That way, I could take the heat off Malcolm. I'd make up a lie that I escaped, slit Malcolm's throat, and ran back to Connor. I could keep Malcolm safe, and maybe, with time, free the other women. It wasn't much of a plan, but it was something. I had to try.

I glanced out the window and saw Malcolm disappear behind the lobby door. I'd have a couple of minutes at best to escape. I had to run. Now.

Unbuckling, I grabbed the car door, I tried to open it, but it was locked.

"Ugh, fucking child locks," I hissed. Climbing to the front, I slipped into the front seat, hit the unlock button, and got out of the car. It was misting and the sky outside was a pale gray. My eyes darted around for a place to hide, and they locked onto the dumpster. There were woods beyond that. Perfect.

I only made it about two feet before large arms were around my waist.

"Where do you think you're going?"

My heart was pounding a mile a minute, thinking I'd been caught by one of Connor's thugs. It was only when I registered Malcolm's voice and felt his arms pressing me close to him that I started to cry.

"Amanda, what is it? What's wrong?" He spun me around so that he could look into my eyes.

"You have to let me go," I whimpered. "I have to go back. He'll kill you if he finds us together. I have to protect you."

"Hey, shh, it's okay," he said. He pulled me into his arms. "You don't need to protect me. I'm protecting you. He's not going to find us. I'll keep you safe, Amanda. I'll keep you safe."

As I wrapped my arms around him and wept onto his shoulder, I swear I felt his lips press softly on the top of my head.

A car pulled into the lot then, and I froze. Malcolm tensed as well until they parked and got out of the car. It was a young woman, dressed in a cleaner's outfit. She glanced over at us, the random couple in the middle of the parking lot. We were drawing attention to ourselves. To try to make our embrace look less like a hostage situation I leaned up and pressed a kiss on Malcolm's lips.

His whole body tensed from my sudden movement. "We're being watched," I whispered against his lips. "Now kiss me back so they don't call the cops on the guy who just ran after a woman fleeing from a black SUV."

The realization of what I was doing kicked in. It was time to play the game of being a happily married couple and not two people on the run from a psycho.

"Right," he said. "So we should probably kiss like we mean it then?"

I nodded once as his eyes locked with mine. I'd given him permission, and judging by the way his gaze darted to my lips, he was game. My heart sped up as he leaned down to kiss me.

MALCOLM

I was having an out-of-body experience. Amanda Jackson wanted me to kiss her. Well, wanted might not be the right word. She needed me to kiss her to not blow our cover as a married couple. Not exactly the same thing as her wanting to kiss me, but looking down at those lush lips, there was no way I'd be able to refuse anything she asked me for at the moment.

Her nod confirmed that she wanted me to kiss her, so there was nothing left to do than grant her wish.

Leaning in, I watched her eyes carefully in case she changed her mind, but her stance didn't waiver. If anything, I could almost swear I saw a hint of desire lingering there.

When our lips pressed together again, I wasn't as stiff as I'd been when she first planted a quick kiss on me. I had not been expecting that. This one I was ready for. As was she.

Her lips were just as soft as I'd imagined them all these years. They yielded to my movements, clinging to me like glue. When her tongue brushed mine, I heard myself let loose a soft moan. Her fingers slid up my neck then latched on to the back of my hair and held on, locking me against her mouth.

Fuck. I understood the hair thing now.

My own hands found their way to her hips. My fingertips dug into her soft curves as I pressed her close to me. This was dangerous. I was enjoying it far more than I should.

Reluctantly, I pushed away, breaking the kiss. She leaned her forehead against mine as we caught our breath.

"We need to go," I whispered.

"I know."

Yet neither one of us moved for a solid minute.

Eventually, it was Amanda who took a deep breath followed by a step back.

"Okay. We can go now," she said. She held out her hand for me to take. I looked down at it, then back at her. In that one gesture, I could tell she was trusting me to keep her safe. To lead her away from the worst of the world.

I took her hand and brought her back to the Tahoe.

Opening the back door, she sighed. "You want me on the floor again, don't you?"

"Just until we're on the highway."

She climbed in and tucked herself against the back passenger seat door.

"Here. So you don't get cold." I yanked off the hoodie from my back. She was shivering as she hadn't gotten dressed yet. She could have easily put on the clothes I packed for her, but there was something about the way she'd curled herself into a little ball that told me she didn't want to move right now.

She took the hoodie and hugged it against her. She brought it to her nose and sniffed.

"It smells like you," she said.

"Should it not?"

A small smile danced across her lips. "No. It's perfect. Thank you."

Nodding, I shut the door and climbed in the front. Time to disappear.

Amanda stayed silent as I pulled out of the parking lot. My eyes scanned around the vehicle every few seconds, anticipating the approach of Connor's thugs. If we were to be found right now, I honestly wasn't sure how much protection I could offer her. I had six rounds at my hip, but the rest of my weapons were in the trunk. While I was an excellent shot at the range, I'd never turned that weapon on someone before. I wouldn't hesitate to pull the trigger, however, if Amanda's life was at risk. Still, I'd be far more secure at the safehouse. Unfortunately, we were about thirty-eight hours away, more than that if we took the side roads. I was starting to rethink if we had time to make it there or if I needed a new plan.

"Are you warm enough?" I asked, reaching for the heat.

"I'm fine."

"We should be safe for you to come up here in a few minutes," I said. "I just want to get some miles behind us first."

"If you need me to stay hidden the whole ride, I'll stay put." There was something off about her. She sounded...scared. As she should be. We were up against a loose cannon who was on the hunt.

"We're going to change cars in the next city. I'll buy a different make and model. We'll take less popular routes. He won't find us."

"And if he does?" she asked. Her voice was barely above a whisper.

"Then I will do everything in my power to protect you. But let's not focus on that right now. For now, I need you to eat something. There should be a bag back there with you. The coffee wasn't ready yet, so I just grabbed a few bottles of water, but there were some muffins that didn't look horrible. I'll make a stop for provisions after we've changed cars. Maybe once we're on the road a bit longer." I checked the mirrors. I'm not sure what I was expecting to find. Perhaps a wave of black SUVs. So far, it was just us and a small silver sedan with a college-aged kid at the wheel. Traffic would pick up, though, once people started their commute to work.

"Isn't buying a car risky? What if he tracks your credit card."

"I'll be paying cash."

"Oh. Right. The go-bag stash. Will that be enough?"

"I'm not going to buy a luxury SUV. I'm gonna find a hunk of junk that will get us to New Hampshire. I want to fly under the radar. I have other vehicles there we can use when we arrive. If I wasn't worried about being tracked, I'd fly us there. But airports, even private ones, mean cameras, and I have no idea where his connections are. Same deal with bus and train stations. Everything is monitored now. That's why I have the Tahoe."

"No, that's smart. He probably has people everywhere. There is a reason no one escapes from him. A reason he's still operating such a massive operation right under people's noses. I mean, seriously, the man is using your name to cover his actions. Talk about balls."

My eyes darted to the back. "My name. What do you mean?"

"Your name is on the building he's using to cage us."

"What?"

"Luxx Apartments & Condos. That's you, right?"

My eyes narrowed. "That fucker. I sold him that building years ago at twice its market value, mostly because it was him who wanted it and you're telling me he's using it to run his human trafficking ring?"

"Sorry."

"That little fuck. I have *nothing* to do with what goes on in that building. You know that right? Jesus? Why the hell would he leave my name on it?"

"Well, I can think of a few reasons. One, you said you

overpriced the sale of the property," Amanda explained, "and that you wouldn't buy a pet from him?"

"I most certainly would not."

She sighed. "Then that's how he nails you down. He keeps your name attached to the building where he's running an illegal operation. You might have sold him the property, but from a public branding perspective, your name is on the building. In that way, he still owns you. If you rat him out for using your name without consent, your name still gets dragged into investigations. Investigations he knows you won't want police looking into."

As much as I hated to admit it, she was right. Connor had me by the balls. It's not like I could sue him without bringing light to both of our illegal activities. The manipulative bastard. That told me two things. He was smart, and he played a long game.

Getting Amanda to the safehouse might not be as easy as I'd anticipated. And even if I did get her there, how long would it take until he found us?

"Eat. We'll be switching transport soon," I said with more confidence than I felt.

CHAPTER FIVE

Connor

While my men were keeping tabs on flights or bus ticket purchases, I opted to take my jet straight to the New Hampshire house. That would give me enough time to get set up and be ready for his arrival. He wouldn't see me coming. If there was so much as a scratch on Amanda, I'd rip his cock off before I killed him and shove it down his throat.

However, if Amanda was in on this escape... *No. Don't even think it*. She'd been kidnapped. Plain and simple. She didn't want to be with Malcolm. She was the victim of this. And I'd bring her back. And what then? Put her back in her cage? Retrain and put her back up for adoption? Unlikely. My dick would demand she stay with me.

"Can I get you anything to drink?" the overly perky flight attendant asked.

"No. Thank you. I need to keep a clear head."

"How about a pillow or a blanket?" Her eyes were flirtatious, as was the way she seemed to push her chest out. I was not unfamiliar with this. Women wanted me. They sensed the danger in me and were compelled by it. But I wasn't in the mood.

"What I need is for you to kindly fuck off," I said.

She blinked, taken aback before she huffed and moved on to the next passenger. I knew I should have chartered a private flight, but I was in a hurry and this commercial flight was the first one out. Before we took off, I sent one final message to Kenny.

> About to take off. I'll hit you up when I land. Text me if you hear anything.

The text was unnecessary, as I knew he'd keep me informed, but I was antsy. Reinforcements were coming by car to see if they could catch them before they made it to New Hampshire. We were boxing them in from both sides. Either way, I'd get him. I'd figure out how much he knew about my operation and then determine what head games he'd played on Amanda to get her to follow him. He must have forced her. No way would she go willingly, knowing what I'd do to her and the other pets if she had.

Once I landed, I'd hit up my East Coast contact. See what additional support I could get. Not that I'd need much. If I got set up before they arrived, Malcolm would just need to open the door to his safehouse, and boom, problem solved.

Glancing at my itinerary, I had one layover in Virginia. I'd make calls then and get my plans sorted. Nodding, I rested my head against the seat. There was little else to do but wait, so I closed my eyes and tried to sleep.

As soon as I drifted off, images of Amanda flashed through my mind. The feeling of her hands digging into my hair; those perfect breasts as she arched her back, begging me to taste; her wanting eyes as they peered into mine.

My cock grew hard at the thought of her. And not just in my dream. *Fuck.* My eyes flung open and confirmed what I was feeling.

Unbuckling my belt, I awkwardly made my way to the bathroom to tend to this beast. I couldn't have my mind clouded when I landed. *Damn, this woman and what she did to me.*

Inside the tiny stall, I undid my belt and let my pants drop to mid-thigh. No way would I let my pants touch this nasty floor. I was rock hard thanks to thoughts of Amanda's tits in my mouth.

With that delicious thought still in my mind, I ran my hand down my length, envisioning her lips there instead.

"Come for me," she begged as my hand worked faster against my dick.

"You want me to come for you?" I whispered. The sound of my strokes seemed to echo inside the small space.

"I need you, Connor. Please." Closing my eyes, I pictured her lips on me again. My hand worked me into a flurry until I came, hard.

"Come for me." Her eyes pleading.

"I just did," I said. I opened my eyes to see my load dripping down the bathroom wall.

"Come save me, Connor."

My blood ran cold. Luxx. She wanted me to save her from Luxx.

"I'm on my way, baby. I'm on my way."

I pulled my pants back up and left the bathroom without cleaning my mess. I had more important things to do. Like plan all the ways I was going to kill Malcolm.

By the time we landed and I made it to my next gate, I checked my phone for messages from Kenny. I was hungry for news. Three messages awaited me.

Security footage of his house shows a Tahoe leaving the property at 3:27 p.m. Approximately thirty minutes after you left. Windows were tinted so we couldn't confirm the number of passengers. We're doing a run of the plates to see if we can track his movements.

Got a sighting of his plates from a video at a toll plaza.

We think they might have pulled off at a rest stop or checked into a hotel for the night. Two cars are staying the course and checking rest stops. I'm checking hotels near the plaza.

Good. This was good. It confirmed my suspicion. He had taken her. It wasn't just a 'drive,' as his assistant insisted. The bastard was trying to pull one over on me. That was his last mistake. His first was stealing from me. He'd pay for both of them.

I sent Kenny a quick text on my burner, letting him know I'd be laid over for the next hour but to keep the updates coming.

It was only a matter of time before I had his neck in my hand. I would relish the sound of it snapping under my fingers. Until then, I needed food.

I glanced out the window. My plane hadn't arrived yet, so I walked over to the restaurant across the gate to order a steak. Bloody. Like Luxx was about to be.

AMANDA

While Malcolm worked the man at the used car lot, I went to use the restroom at the convenience store right next door. Malcolm wanted me to wait for him, but my bladder wasn't having it.

When I got out of the stall, I went to the sink to wash my hands and noticed one of the workers there with a compact. She was doing her best to hide a shiner.

"Arnica gel works pretty well on bruises," I offered.

The woman looked over at me. In her eyes, I could tell she was ashamed she'd been seen trying to cover up that she'd been abused.

"Thanks. Slipped down the stairs," she offered.

The fingerprints around her wrist told a different story.

I nodded. "I've 'fallen down' a few stairs in my life, too. Until one day, I got tired of being so stupid. Constantly falling down the same stairs. I packed my shit and decided to find a different house."

The woman looked at me through the mirror, understanding my not-so-subtle analogy. "Did you find a better place?" the woman asked. She couldn't be more than twenty-one. Still so young. Still finding her way.

"That's the thing about moving," I said. "It's a gamble. Sometimes you trade a set of faulty stairs for a front door that you keep smacking your head into. But sometimes, sometimes, you find a house that doesn't seem to hurt you every time you walk inside it."

"That would be nice." She sighed.

I placed a tentative hand on her shoulder. "You deserve a nice home. A safe home."

She nodded once, then went back to putting on her makeup.

When I left the bathroom, Malcolm was there, perched like an eagle ready to kill.

"Jesus, you scared me," I said. His hulking figure was standing right in front of the door.

"We have a new ride. Let's grab some food and get moving." He placed his hand on the small of my back and put me slightly in front of him as though to protect me from the couple looking at beer behind us.

"Can we get Doritos? Like the real ones? Sam used to only let me buy the generic because they were cheaper, and they are *not* the same thing."

"Doritos?" Malcolm raised an eyebrow. "I haven't had those since I was a kid."

"So at least three bags then." I grabbed a shopping basket from one of the holding pins by the door.

"Get whatever you want, just be quick about it. Maybe try to select a few items with some nutritional value. It might be all we get for the next few days."

"I'll have you know Doritos have corn *and* cheese. Two of the major food groups."

Less than twenty minutes later, we had five plastic bags of food in the back seat of the maroon Jetta he bought. The thing had rust along all four doors, one of which was blue, but the dealer had assured Malcolm that it would take us to Florida. Malcolm didn't give our real destination to the man because, well, Connor.

The car was significantly smaller than the Tahoe and had no tinted windows. The back was so small that I couldn't even fit on the floor so, reluctantly, Malcolm succumbed to letting me ride beside him as long as I wore the hat and sunglasses he'd picked up at the store. The hat was a bright white baseball cap with some sports team logo I didn't know plastered on the front, while the sunglasses were so big they covered up nearly half of my face, which I supposed was the point.

Tucking all of my now-black hair up into the hat, I frowned in the small mirror on the back of the visor.

"Well, this is attractive."

"I'm not exactly thrilled with my look, either." Malcolm too was sporting a different baseball cap, but his cap was blue and plain, with the brim flipped to the back. He sported gold-framed sunglasses with a yellow tint. He'd ditched his button-up shirt for just the white T-shirt underneath.

"At least you still look hot," I grumbled. "I look like I'm on my way to a casino with my rent money."

Malcolm's lip twitched slightly in apparent amusement.

"You think it's funny I look awful?"

He shook his head. "No. It's not that. You are still stunning, even if you do resemble the Wish version of Vanilla Ice. What has me smirking is your comment that you think *this*," he gestured to his attire, "is in any way 'hot.'"

I shrugged. "I like what I like. Don't shame me for it."

His face grew serious for a moment. "You're right. I'm sorry. Drool away," he said.

I laughed despite myself.

Once we'd put a few miles behind us, and I trusted that the Jetta wasn't going to fall apart, I relaxed a bit. I noticed Malcolm was still keeping a watchful eye out for any cars behind us. Something told me though that if Connor's men were following, we'd never know it.

"Can I ask you a question?" Malcolm asked.

"Sure."

"Earlier, when you were in the back seat of the Tahoe..."

"Yeah?"

He looked over at me. "You seemed a little lost in thought. You okay?"

Wow. He'd picked up on that? I hadn't realized I was so transparent. But that was just it. I wasn't. No one ever knew what I was really thinking.

"How so?" I challenged.

"I don't know. You just seemed...scared, I suppose. Which is understandable. I guess I want to make sure you know that I'm here. If you need to talk."

Nailed it in one. That was a first. "Um. Yeah. I *was* scared. If we're being honest here, I was contemplating if I should have tried to run when we stopped again."

"Amanda, I thought we—"

"I know. I know," I said, cutting him off. "It's just...I started thinking about what would happen if Connor caught up to us. What he'd think when he saw us together. If he'd even bother to ask any questions before putting a bullet into our brains. If I went back to him, then at the very least you wouldn't be in danger anymore."

"Amanda, you can't go back there." His voice was firm, yet also pained. He wasn't ordering me to stay. He was begging me.

"I won't." I was resolved.

"Are you just saying that to appease me?" he asked. Rightfully so.

I shook my head. "No. I mean it. While I was in the bathroom, back at the store. A woman was there. One of the cashiers. She was covering up a bruise...and I don't know. I just saw myself. I *was* her. For so many years. I didn't see a way out of it. I didn't know any other way." I looked over at him. "I can see now that not all men are cruel. That may prove to be yet another mistake, trusting you, but that's what I'm doing,

Malcolm. I'm trusting you to keep me safe. To keep us both safe."

"I will, Amanda." He reached over and took my hand, and I let him. "And once you're safe, I *will* find a way to take his whole operation down."

I let loose a breath. Of the impossible odds we were up against, taking down Connor's business seemed like a tall order. But that wasn't today's problem. Today's problem was getting to the safehouse before this car fell apart.

CHAPTER SIX

Connor

"Yes, I understand that there is a Category three storm happening *in Florida*. What I don't understand is how that storm affects me here in Virginia!" I shouted at the airline front desk receptionist. The receptionist remained unbothered.

"As I said on the announcements, sir, your connecting flight into New Hampshire is currently in Florida, and due to said storm, that plane is grounded. I can get you a voucher for the hotel, or I can see when our next available flight is—"

I didn't wait for her to finish. I'd rent a car. If there were even any left. Hurricane Fucking Humberto could suck my left nut.

My sour mood was only getting worse by the moment, especially when I realized in the parking garage back at the airport in Seattle that I'd not be able to bring my guns. Not sure what I was thinking trying to get through TSA with my go-bag. I'd have to get new weapons when we landed. Irritating.

With my much lighter go-bag back in my hand, I made it over to the rental place. After about forty minutes of waiting, I was able to secure a rental. Large tips generally got me what I wanted in public situations. The gun worked every other time. Once I was in the car, I called Carlos. One of my men was stationed in Seattle.

"Change of plans. I'm driving. My flight was canceled due to a storm. ETA will be later, but I should still make it before them to make preparations. Also, I'll need a weapon when I arrive. Any news?"

"We found his Tahoe."

"Where?" My hands curled around the steering wheel.

"It was sold to some rinky-dink used car lot in Idaho. They sold it the same day. Man doesn't remember who he sold it to."

"Help him remember," I said. "I want to know the make and model of the car Malcolm bought. Understood?"

"I thought you'd say that. We're pulling up to his residence now. I'll call you with the information."

Satisfied I'd get my answers, I turned the key and started the eleven-hour drive to New Hampshire. While the drive was a kink in my plans, it hadn't derailed the endgame. I'd still arrive well before the two of them if they continued to drive across the country. My guess was that Malcolm wouldn't be stupid enough to use public transportation. Too many sets of eyes to spot them. Which meant I'd have about twenty-four hours, give or take, to prepare.

As it stood now, I had a few options. First, I could arrive, hide on the grounds, and the moment Malcolm was in my sight, stick a bullet in his head. Clean. Simple. Effective. That would be a foolish play, however. One made out of rage.

Better to be rational. Arrive at the house, set up surveillance, then observe them. Make them feel like they had outsmarted me. Allow them to let their guard down, and then go in for the kill. I needed to know how much Amanda was involved in this choice to run and how much Malcolm knew about my operation. What was known would determine Amanda's fate. I wanted to know the truth, not concocted lies in a fearful confession to tell me what I wanted to hear.

Just then, my phone vibrated.

Kenny's at the NH house.

Kenny had taken a redeye after we'd departed earlier. I typed a quick reply to have him call me.

A minute later, my phone was ringing.

"Are they there yet?" I asked.

"Nope. Just me and some trees. I parked a mile away and hoofed it."

"Good," I said. "What can you tell me about his setup?"

"It's tight. It's even got invisible fencing to detect movement. I'm guessing, like, a good 500 feet from the house. I haven't gotten too close, as I don't want to trip any sensors, but it looks like he's pretty well set up from what I can tell."

"Fuck." Of course he'd have set up good security. The dick. "What does he have for a power source? Can we cut stuff?"

"Looks like solar. And the generator is within the fence. Let me think a bit on that."

"Think fast. They will likely be there shortly. Can you set up camp somewhere nearby?"

"Yep. You want me to call if I see them or just take care of things?"

"Call me. I'm headed your way now. I'll be there in about ten hours or so. I want to handle this one personally. Understood? No one touches the girl until I know what she's blabbed."

"You got it."

I hung up with Kenny and pressed on the gas.

MALCOLM

At some point during our drive, Amanda drifted off to sleep. How she was able to sleep with the sound of the rattling of this hunk of junk, I'd never understand, but she was likely bone tired after such an ordeal.

So far there weren't any cars following us that I could make out, but I didn't want to risk being seen. Truth be told, I was already contemplating making another car swap. If only to save my brain from jostling around so much. Or maybe we'd risk it and take the train. I could try to find someone to pay for our tickets, then we could board without much fanfare. If we went to a small enough town to board, there probably wouldn't even be cameras.

At this rate, we'd never get there. And I needed her safe. Now.

"I have to pee," came the sound of a grumpy Amanda.

My lips curled into a smile. "There's a rest stop in a few miles. I could use it too."

"Probably no real food there?"

"I'm sure there's a vending machine..."

"I'd kill for Olive Garden. Hell, just the salad and breadsticks and I'd be happy."

"Olive Garden. Really? Why do women love that place so much?"

"What? I like carbs. Sue me," she huffed. "And when are you going to let me drive? I'm sick of being the passenger."

"Fine. We can shift after the rest stop. Happy?"

She fist-pumped the sky. "Finally, we can go past sixty."

"No. No, Amanda. We can't speed. If we get pulled over, Connor could track us. Plus, this car might fall apart if we went that fast."

She sighed. "Right. This sucks."

"I know what would make it better."

"Oh?" She wiggled her eyebrows.

I nodded toward one of the road signs.

"Ah! There's an Olive Garden!"

"We'll see if they do carry out. We can't take the time to stop though."

"Oh, my God! Thank you!"

Turning my head, I looked over at her to smile, but she surprised me with a kiss. A kiss I think she'd intended to land on my cheek instead of my lips because she instantly apologized.

"Sorry." She blushed before throwing her eyes down at the floor.

"No. It's fine. If I'd known that was all it took to get a kiss from you, I would have taken you to Olive Garden in high school."

Her embarrassment seemed to shift into amusement as her lips curled into a small smile. "You know, it's so strange that of all the people in the world Connor wanted to sell me to, it ended up being you. Do you think that's a coincidence or..."

"What?" I raised an eyebrow. "Fate?"

She looked at me with big eyes but then shrugged. "You don't think so?"

"Do I think it's fate that led us both down horrific individual tragedies only to align us together years later as the target of a monster?"

"Well when you put it like that," she sighed.

I could tell that my answer had disappointed her, so I tried to explain myself. "I'm sorry. I'm not much of a romantic when it comes to things like fate. I'm not much of a romantic period. I haven't exactly had the best role models for what love looks like."

"Yeah. Same." Her eyebrows pinched together. "You're right. Fate is the wrong word. Maybe it was serendipity?"

"Serendipity?"

"Yeah. It's like an unplanned but fortunate discovery. That's us. Unplanned but fortunate."

My lips tugged into a reluctant smile. "Okay. I'll allow that," I said. I turned into the restaurant parking lot.

"How are we doing this?" Amanda asked as I found a spot.

Killing the engine, I did a lookout to see if anyone pulled in after us. When I was satisfied we hadn't been followed, I removed the key and undid my seatbelt. "I'll go in and order the takeout. In three minutes, you come in to use the restroom. Come straight back to the car and lock it." He handed me the keys. "Keep your head as low as you can and keep your hat and glasses on."

"Even inside?"

"Especially then. That's where the cameras will be, if any."

"Fine," I sighed, pulling down the brim of my hat.

"I'll come out as soon as the food is ready. Speak to no one."

"I want the fettuccine alfredo with chicken since you're buying. Don't forget the breadsticks," she added before I stepped out of the car.

The doors locked behind me as I nodded to Amanda. Keeping my head low, I walked into the restaurant to place our order.

"Your order will be ready in about twenty minutes," the hostess with a plastered-on smile said before she moved on to the next person waiting in line.

Since there was nothing to do but wait, I took that time to use the washroom. The giant clock hanging on the wall indicated Amanda should be coming in soon if she listened to my instructions. I waited for a few moments after I got out of the bathroom, pretending to look at my phone, but really I was waiting for her.

I was debating opening the women's bathroom door to see if she'd made it inside yet, when I noticed her walking toward me. Head bowed as I'd instructed.

Putting my phone in my back pocket, I walked back toward the front, whispering only a "Good girl," when she passed me.

I took a seat in the waiting area where I could see the restrooms. Not that I thought she'd run off again, but I wanted to be sure. A few minutes later she came out, cheeks flushed, but gaze fixed on the ground. She glanced up at me once, and I couldn't help but smile that she had sought out my eyes. In a flash, she was back on track and heading to the car. As casually as I could, I watched from the window. I let slip a sigh of relief when the door closed behind her.

Using the time, I opted to check in with Camila. I sent her a quick text on the burner.

Updates? M

For several minutes there was no reply, but then there came a thirty-second video clip along with a text.

> This was sent to your place via FedEx three hours ago. The security cameras alerted me it was there. It was an envelope with a tablet inside. It had a sticky on it that said, 'Hit play'.

I checked the time, there were still at least ten minutes before the food was ready. I signaled to the woman at the desk that I was stepping out to make a call. Turning my volume low and angling myself so no one outside could see the video, I hit play. I fought hard not to throw up.

"Oh, Malcolm. Didn't your mother ever tell you not to touch other people's toys?" Connor's face wasn't in the frame, but I knew it was his voice. A second later a woman came into the shot. She had tears streaking down her face. Connor held up her hand and slid a cigar cutter over her pinkie.

"Do you see this?" Connor was saying against the sound of the woman's cries. "This is what I'm going to do to your dick for stealing what's mine." In an instant, the woman's finger was severed.

The video cut off and my stomach lurched.

Camila texted.

> How much longer until you get to the safehouse?

> Going as fast as I can. I'm driving straight through.

> Good. Txt when there. And M, if he shows up… kill him. Kill the bastard.

> I will.

And I meant it.

CHAPTER SEVEN

Amanda

Walking from the restaurant to wait in the car for our food, I had only one thought in my head: Malcolm was an asshole. Of all the things he could have whispered in my ear inside, he had to choose to say, "Good girl." Sent a goddamn chill right down to my lady bits. I'd always known I had a bit of a praise kink, but until I heard him whisper that phrase to me in his deep, husky voice, I wasn't positive. Now I was. I was wet and insanely horny. How was I supposed to sit beside that man feeling like this for hours on end? There was only one thing to do. And I needed to do it before he got back.

Checking my surroundings, I grabbed Malcolm's suit jacket from the back and draped it over my lap. Sliding my hands under the coat, I undid my jeans and yanked them over my bare ass. The pleather seat felt cold against my bare bottom, but I didn't care. I needed release and I needed it now.

Eager fingers plunged into my seam. Fuck, I was wet. My middle finger began the small circles against my clit as my mouth opened to pant.

Malcolm's eyes danced in my mind. *"Good girl. Come for me."* The moan that escaped my lips was louder than I expected, but I didn't suppress it. In my mind, I observed him as he watched me working myself into a frenzy. It was wildly erotic. Then he smiled. The way he had inside the restaurant. That was it. I came apart, screaming through my orgasm.

A second later, the driver's side door flew open and Malcolm was there, hand on his weapon, eyebrows pinched together in rage, then confusion.

"Malcolm! Jesus!" I shrieked, pulling the jacket tighter around my waist.

"You were screaming," he said. He looked in the backseat and then at me.

"I was coming," I muttered. I reached down to pull my pants back up.

"Coming?" He watched as I fought to get back into my pants. "Oh. Right. Um. Sorry. I'll just..." He shut the car door and stood with his back against the window.

Sighing, I tossed his jacket in the back and redid my pants.

"I'm decent," I yelled.

He stood outside a moment before he got in. He handed me the bag of food, which was warm against my lap and smelled like garlic and happiness.

"Sorry... I didn't mean to interrupt."

He was clearly mortified. For some reason, that made me grin.

"You didn't interrupt. I finished."

"Oh. Well, good. Because we need to move. Now." He started the car and peeled out of the parking lot. His whole body seemed tense. I tried to meet his eyes but he wouldn't look at me and kept his eyes on the road. He appeared spooked. My blood ran cold.

"What happened? Were we spotted?"

"Let me get on the highway. And duck down."

Connor found us. It had to be that. There was no other reason for Malcolm to be this tense or for me to hide this far away from where we left.

Ducking down into the seat so that my head was no longer visible, my heart thundered in my chest. *How? How could he have found us? We'd been so careful.*

I wanted to ask him a million questions, but I could tell he needed to focus on nothing but the road. Whatever happened inside that restaurant was enough to have him running scared. If Malcolm was scared, then there had to be a good reason.

He didn't say a word for about five minutes. Neither did I. I stayed crouched in an uncomfortable position, feeling the vibrations of the vehicle in my spine until Malcolm finally spoke.

"Okay. I don't think we're being followed. Nor do I think he knows where we are," he said. "But...he knows we left. And he's not happy. He sent a warning." Malcolm handed me his phone. "Hit play."

Taking the phone, I sat up a little higher and watched in horror as Kelli's pinky was removed.

"Oh, my god." Bile rose in my throat. "He's punishing them for my escape."

"It's a power play. He wants us running scared. I don't think he knows how far we've already gotten. Which is good. Even still, I'm going to drive through the night. We're getting you to the safehouse first thing in the morning."

"And in the meantime, Kelli loses all her fingers?"

Malcolm didn't answer. He kept his eyes on the road.

"You have to bring me back," I whispered. "Dump me somewhere close. I'll find the way back and you won't be spotted."

"Absolutely not."

"He'll kill her. He'll kill her out of spite."

"If you go back, he'll just kill you as well. There is nothing I can do about your friend while we are in this car. But once we get to the safehouse, I have access to my resources. I'll find a way to get her out. To get them all out. But I won't sacrifice your life to do it. Understood?"

He was right. I knew he was right. But that didn't change the guilt that I felt for what Kelli had just endured because of me.

"I don't think he'll kill her," I said after a moment. "She's worth too much to him alive. The fact that she's defective now probably cost him a fortune. I know he had a buyer already lined up for her."

Malcolm watched my expression carefully. "What do you know about his operation? Any details I might be able to use to bring him down?"

"There's not much to tell other than what I already mentioned. He lures women in with a false ad for housing. He asked a bunch of questions during the walk-through. Questions I know now were designed to determine if I had family that would miss me. Once he gets us in the unit, it's as good as over. He gives them a moment to look over the lease, and once he's in the hall, he locks us in. After that, he will housebreak the 'pets,' as he calls them, and send out adoption papers—"

"What does he do to housetrain them?" He sounded appropriately disturbed by the sentence he had spoken.

"I don't know. My training was sort of skipped because the window to sell me to you was so short."

Malcolm shook his head. "All the times that man sent me 'adoption' papers... I never once considered that he'd enslaved these women. I always assumed it was an elongated escort system. I know men who have them, but most of them are married, so I thought they were permanent side pieces. I sincerely believed the women were being compensated for their services. I didn't know they took ownership of a human. That's just..."

"Fucked up?"

"Yes."

"Were you never tempted by the adoption papers?"

Malcolm turned to look at me. "I never opened any files he sent me. Well, not after I saw the very first 'application to adopt' he had couriered over to me. I had no idea what was inside the envelope. I thought it had something to do with the sale of the building. I had my assistants burn any future correspondence with him."

The guilt of all of the events that had transpired in the last few days was weighing on me. First Kelli, now Malcolm? How many people were going to get hurt because I made a stupid decision to answer an ad that was too good to be true?

"Tell me what security he has there. What does the setup look like?"

I let free a breath. "It's pretty high-tech. Thumbprint sensors on the doors, on the elevators, so even if we did manage to escape, we couldn't get down the elevator."

"Smart," Malcolm grumbled.

"The cages themselves are, from the outside, normal-looking apartment doors, but they have facial recognition to be let in. Thumbprint scans on the door to get out too. Inside the cage, there are cameras in every room mounted to the ceiling so he can watch you whenever he wants. I was on the thirteenth floor, so jumping wasn't an option, even if you could manage to break the tinted glass, which you couldn't."

"Did you try to break it?"

I frowned at him. "With what? You're not getting it. There wasn't anything inside to break the glass with. All the furniture was bolted down. Anything that might be used as a weapon was gone."

"Clever bastard," he muttered. "Okay, what *was* in the unit?"

I shrugged. "Not much. Just a mattress on the floor in the bedroom. No bedding. Not even a pillow. Nothing in the closets or bathroom. No shower curtain. The dining room had a table and chairs, but they were bolted to the floor. Living room furniture was bolted too. There was a couch and two chairs." I shivered thinking about the red chair.

"What?" Malcolm asked, noticing that my demeanor had changed.

"Nothing... It's just. He had this red wingback chair he made us sit in. Kelli had one too. When he came into the room, you had to sit in that chair, legs crossed, arms on the armrests."

"You never made a run for it when he opened the door?"

Did he seriously think I hadn't considered that? "Firstly, the chair was a good ten feet away from the door, so even if I did somehow manage to get by him in the two seconds it takes him to lock the door, then what?"

He blinked at me. "You keep running."

"To where? The elevator? The one that has a thumbprint scan on it? As does the stairwell exit. Not to mention the woman at the front who would alert Connor's goons the second she saw me. Trying to escape would not only ensure my death, but now it looks like it also ensured the others are punished for it too."

I was disgusted with myself. By letting Malcolm take me I'd put all of them in danger. I was a horrible person. That should have been me being punished. Not Kelli.

Looking down at my lap, I felt the warm bag of Olive Garden still waiting for us. Inside the bag, I knew it held my favorite pasta dish and that delicious garlic bread. But, despite my protesting stomach, all I could think about was how the breadsticks reminded me of fingers...and then Kelli's finger being severed— Suddenly, I had no appetite.

The reality of the danger I was in became abundantly clear now. It might have sounded ridiculous, but once we crossed the state line, I thought the odds of him bothering to waste his time and money on finding us would diminish. He had a business to run. He couldn't waste his time or energy on one escaped stray. Yes, he'd be angry, but if we were long gone, what could he do besides chase us for a few days? Once we got to the safehouse, the trail would grow cold. I couldn't think about what happened then. My plans for the future were done by the day and not beyond that.

Now it was real. He knew we were gone. And he was making it personal. The wondering what he'd do when he found out we'd left wasn't hypothetical anymore. It was a reality. He discovered we were missing days earlier than we had planned. Our lead time was drastically reduced. We were supposed to be long hidden before Connor even caught wind we'd left. Instead, we had a few hours of lead time at best. Worst off, Connor made this personal. He wasn't going to let this go. He, and who knows how many of his goons, were hunting us, and I was no longer convinced we could outrun them.

MALCOLM

I could see that she was beating herself up about what Connor had done to that woman. That she felt guilty for something he did. It was disgusting how that man's behavior affected Amanda's emotions. But that was his profession. Brainwashing. Making the women feel like they deserved the treatment they received from their new owners. I wanted to turn around and find Connor and cut him from limb to limb for what he had done to her. That level of abuse would take years to recover from. If ever.

"Amanda, look at me."

She struggled to pick her eyes up from where they'd landed on her lap. Her hands had twisted themselves up around her waist like she was nauseous. Our food, now growing cold at her feet.

"This isn't your fault. Okay? None of it," I said.

She refused to look at me but instead gave her attention to the world whizzing by us outside. "Isn't it though? If I hadn't let you take me—"

"But you didn't," I corrected. "You only came with me because you thought I was bringing you back to Connor. If anything, I kidnapped you after Connor did."

"That's not—"

I held up a finger. "That is *exactly* the story you tell. If we are separated somehow... If he finds you... If anything happens to me... *That* is the story you tell. *I kidnapped you.* I held you at gunpoint and threatened to expose his business if you didn't come quietly. He needs to believe that you were protecting him."

"But—"

"I don't care what happens to me, Amanda. I need to make

sure you stay alive. Besides, it's not that far off from the truth. I did take you against your will, and I do have a gun..."

"So you want me to throw you under the bus?"

"If we're captured? Yes. One hundred percent. All that matters to me is that you are unharmed."

"Except you die in that scenario. That doesn't work for me."

"Amanda—"

"'Your plan won't work anyway. He won't believe that you kidnapped me."

"He will if he thinks you love him."

She popped her head around to stare at me.

"If what you said about how he treated you differently than his other pets is true," I continued, "he might have feelings of his own for you. After seeing that video, I can assure you that's not a man without some skin in the game. His eyes gave him away. I didn't see a man who was angry about stolen property. I saw point-blank jealousy. He was pissed another man had you. And in that show of emotion, he's let me see his hand. He's jeopardizing his entire operation to come after you. You and I both know he wouldn't do that for any of those other women. Sure, he might send a few guys to hunt her down, but Connor is personally invested in this chase. That tells me that he *wants* to believe you didn't leave him. He *wants* to believe he's rescuing you. So, if he finds us...if it looks like there is no other option...make him believe he was right."

"I'm not going to sacrifice your life for mine," Amanda said. Her eyebrows pinched together in determination.

"No matter what happens. Convince him that you love him. Okay? Promise me, or I'll pull over right now."

She let free a long sigh and traced a finger down the glass. "Okay. I promise. It wouldn't be the first time I've had to pretend to love someone to protect myself from being hurt. Hell, it's the only kind of love that I know."

I hated that was her reality.

"It's fine. Maybe someone like me isn't meant to know what

real love feels like anyway. I mean, not to be twisted, but Connor probably came the closest to love as I had ever gotten."

I'm not sure why, but that comment upset me. "What do you mean by that?"

"It's a great question. One I don't have the answer to myself. I know that what I felt for Connor wasn't love. But there was definitely an attraction. My body responded to his. Which is very confusing for me to reconcile in my mind. I mean, yes, there is probably some merit to the self-preservation thing. Giving in to his demands meant he might not kill me. A person would be willing to do anything to stay alive. It makes sense. Hell, even the idea of trying to develop feelings for your abuser so the trauma of what they do to you doesn't mess you up so much." She lowered her head in shame. "But I don't think that's what happened with us. I think it's more twisted than that."

"How so?"

She didn't answer for a moment, but I could see she was formulating her thoughts, so I gave her time. Finally, she spoke.

"I read somewhere that people accept the love they feel they deserve. Maybe it's as simple as that. The type of love I deserve is the way Connor treated me. Toxic. Abusive. Self-serving."

My eyes darted over to see her in the seat beside me. She'd pulled her knees up to her chest and was hugging them. She looked so utterly broken in body and spirit. I both hated and understood that level of self-loathing.

"When my mother was dating that dirtbag," I said, "I found myself getting angry at her for being so stupid. Couldn't she see how poorly he was treating her? Why didn't she just walk away from him? As an adult, I understand more about how an abuser's mind works. How they manipulate their target. How they corrupt the person's self-worth. Once I understood the behavior, I started to see it everywhere. And in my line of work, the power dynamics are always at play. Someone always has the power and someone else wants it. I see married colleagues all the time professing that they were madly in love, and then the next week see one of them in the arms of another person. It made me realize that people are selfish. They take what they want. Sex. Power. Money. Love? Please. That's a made-up word. No one I've ever met has truly been in love. In lust maybe, but not love. Being in love means you care about something more than yourself.

"What I'm trying to say, poorly, I might add, is that I don't think you love Connor. Nor do I think he loves you. I think he is a master manipulator and took advantage of your vulnerabilities. If he can control your thoughts, he can control you. You can't blame yourself for trying to survive an unthinkable situation. You did what you needed to. Whether you did it consciously or not. That said, I do think there is some truth to that idea of accepting the love we deserve. Maybe I don't deserve it either."

She gnawed at her bottom lip with her teeth for a moment. "Pull the car over."

"What?"

"Pull the car over. Now."

I raised an eyebrow. "Is something wrong?"

"Yes. I need you to pull over. Right the fuck now."

Confused, I looked in the rearview mirror and turned on the blinker to pull over. A small culvert to the side of the highway put us off the road far enough to not be in danger of being hit. Rush hour had passed, but there were still plenty of cars on the road.

When the car came to a stop she reached over and turned the keys, killing the engine.

"Amanda? What is it? What's wrong?"

"I want to blow you. Right here. Right now."

"What? What are you talking about? Where is this coming from?"

"You're lonely. I'm lonely. We're both adults. We don't have to feel like this."

"Amanda—"

"Look, I get it that you don't want to take advantage of me. But can you let *me* take advantage of *you*?"

"Now is not really the time for—"

"You don't get it. I need to feel something other than this terror that's spinning inside my head right now. All I can think about is Kelli and how much pain she must be in. And how I am going to be next. I don't want to feel this anymore. I need to feel something other than scared." Her eyes pleaded with me. "Please, Malcolm. I need an escape. Even if it's temporary."

It was the pleading in her eyes that had me dropping all of my resolve.

"I'll tell you what," I began, pondering my words very carefully. "I will agree to let you give me head *only* because I'm starting not to be able to think straight with you beside me and I can't afford a misstep in my logic. But, Amanda, that's where it ends. I am *not* having sex with you."

"I know." She lowered her head. "You're not interested in me like that."

"Damn it, woman. That's not it at all. I'm not going to have sex with you because *when* we make love, I want there to be no trace of obligation or fear or any doubt in your mind that having sex with me is what you want to do."

At that, Amanda's head lifted. A slight smile danced on her lips. "When we make love?"

"Yes, Amanda. *When*. Not if."

We would become one, of that I had no doubt, but not now. Not until the threat of Connor was well out of her mind. There could be no sense of obligation on her end. I didn't care if that took months or years. When we share a bed someday it would be because she wanted to.

"So...no penetration, but oral. Is that the deal?"

"That's the deal, Amanda. Take it or leave it."

Licking her lips, she said, "I'll take it."

He nodded. "Okay."

CHAPTER EIGHT

Amanda

Okay? I still couldn't fathom it. He'd said "okay" to my giving him oral. I was finally going to be able to taste this delicious man. What I had told him was a hundred percent true. I knew I used sex as a way to escape uncomfortable situations with men in the past, but this time... I genuinely wanted to touch him. Feel him. Taste him.

In my excitement, I reached my hand down to get started but he stopped it with his hand.

"Not here. It's too dangerous. We might be seen. Reported."

"I don't care," I said. I was surprised by how husky my voice sounded.

"Amanda, no. I won't risk it. I'll pull over at the next exit. I'll get us a hotel. I'm not going to let the first time you touch me be in a beat-up Jetta."

"The first time? Are you implying there will be others?" I smirked.

He frowned. "You know what I mean. If we do this, we're doing it on a bed. With privacy. Or we don't do it at all."

I lifted my hands in surrender and moved my hands back to my lap. "Find us a bed then. Fast."

His eyes darkened as he gazed at me, and damn did it make me hungry for him. He nodded once before he pulled back onto the highway.

Fortunately for both of us, there was a hotel less than ten minutes away from where we had pulled over. Malcolm went in by himself to get a room, and while he was inside, I thought about Connor and what he'd do to the both of us if he knew what was about to happen. A shiver ran down my body. Maybe this was a stupid idea? Maybe stopping was dumb. Was my libido about to put us in horrible danger?

Malcolm came out then, hat pulled down low. It made him look sexy as hell. Fuck it. Might as well have some fun before Connor killed us. He pointed to my hat that was on the back seat. Sighing, I grabbed the hat and pulled it over my head, doing my best to tuck as much of my hair inside it as I could.

He locked the car door and took my hand. The gesture startled me, but I didn't pull away. His hand was strong over mine. Warm.

"We're in room 211."

"Room sixty-nine wasn't available?" I teased.

He didn't answer me but walked faster. I couldn't help wondering if planting the seed of sixty-nine had put a little pep in his step.

When we got to the room, Malcolm inserted the key card, but nothing happened. He tried it again and again, jamming it in and out of the slot.

I grabbed the card from his hands. "That's no way to treat a lady," I scolded. "You don't just jackhammer your way in and expect her to open. You need to go nice and slow."

I inserted the card gently and the green light signaled. "Like so."

"Smart ass." He gestured for me to go first. Knowing he was looking at my backside as I went into the room, I reached up to the waistband of my sweats and lowered them so he could see the top of my ass.

"Amanda! Jesus," he whispered, shoving me inside and closing the door behind us. "Someone could have seen you."

"Not with your hulking frame behind me. You easily cover two of me." I pulled my pants back up and smirked at him before I turned into the room. There wasn't much to see. A king-sized bed with a horrific floral pattern, two end tables, lamps straight out of the seventies, and dark curtains closing off the daylight.

I hopped on the bed and giggled. "This will do just fine," I said. I patted the spot beside me. Malcolm didn't budge from the hallway. "What's wrong? Are you scared of me?"

Malcolm looked me dead in the eye. "Yes."

His reply took me aback.

"Why?"

"Amanda, it's no secret that I've had a massive crush on you since high school. I've dreamt about doing this with you for years."

I stood up and wrapped my arms around his waist.

"And now you can. So what's the problem?" I whispered.

He clenched his jaw and took the smallest of steps back. Not enough to break the connection, but one that told me he was uncomfortable.

"Are you scared of what Connor's reaction will be if he finds out?" I asked.

He looked up at me, clearly annoyed.

"What? No. Of course not. I don't give a fuck what Connor thinks about me." At that, he pulled free of my arms and ran his hands through his buzzed hair, almost as though he'd forgotten his locks were no longer there to take his frustration out on.

"What is it then? Are you a virgin or something?"

"I'm not a virgin, Amanda. Far from it."

That was both a relief and slightly annoying to hear at the same time.

"So, what's the deal? Why are you scared? Afraid I have an STD or something?"

That earned me another glare. "No, it's not that. I'm scared that if we do this...I'll never want to let you go."

"Who said you had to?" The words slipped out of my mouth without any hesitation.

His eyes grew dark as his focus darted to my lips. His hands grasped my hips hard as we pressed our foreheads together.

"Don't tease me with words you think I want to hear."

"I would never tease you." I put my hand on his balls. His erection sprang to life through his pants. "Well, maybe a little teasing."

He let loose a groan. He stopped my hand where it was, cupping him. "Are you sure?" he asked. His voice was strained. Almost like he was doing everything he could to restrain himself until I gave him full permission.

"Yes, Malcolm. I want this. I want you. Now fucking kiss me already."

He took one small inhalation, before his lips, finally, touched mine.

MALCOLM

Ever since our staged kiss in the parking lot, I had been dreaming of a moment when our lips would lock again. Her hand on my balls and her body pressed to mine, I could hardly believe it was real.

Her free hand quickly found the back of my hair again. Eager fingers dug into my strands, locking me to her. Not that I had any plans of breaking the kiss.

I kept one hand locked on her hips, but my other hand inched up her side, knowing where it wanted to go but nervous if I would be allowed.

"My God, Malcolm, stop torturing me and touch my breasts already." She let go of my hair and grabbed my hand hovering between us. With force, she shoved it over her breast. The sound that came out of my mouth was slightly embarrassing.

"Fuck me," I whispered.

"I'm trying to." She giggled. She let me explore her breasts over her shirt while she rubbed her fingers up and down my pants, torturing my cock.

After a moment, she took a step back from me, breaking our connection. "Close your eyes," she said.

I was willing to do anything she wanted. So I closed my eyes. There was the sound of the rustle of fabric. Maybe she was getting the bed ready? My cock twitched at the thought of it.

"Okay. You can open them now."

Lifting my lids, I quickly discovered that it wasn't the bed she had undressed, but herself. She stood in front of me, naked and wanting. A goddess, waiting to be ravished.

"Breathtaking," I whispered. And she was. The most stunning creature I'd ever seen. Far better than the versions of her I'd imagined over the years.

"Your turn," she said, nodding at my clothes.

Now was not the time to be bashful. I took a step back and took off my shirt. Then, I removed my belt and started to undo my zipper.

"No," she whispered.

I glanced up at her, wondering if she'd changed her mind.

"On second thought, I want to take him out." She grinned.

Hot damn.

She reached for my zipper and pulled it down painfully slow. Then, with a bit of maneuvering, I was out of my pants with my cock firmly in her hands.

"Well, hello again." She smiled at my cock.

I was about to say something, but before I could, her lips were around me. Her sudden warmth against me caused me to see literal stars.

"Fuck," I grunted.

She responded by cupping my balls. But the combination of her lips, tongue, and hands against me like that, combined with literal years of dreaming of this very moment, and well, I came. I'd lasted all of two minutes with her lips on me.

"Shit. Sorry."

She pulled her mouth off me, swallowing me down with a smile. "Don't be. I'm flattered I was able to get you off so fast."

I held a hand out to help her back up to standing. "Well, it doesn't take much when it comes to you. Just thinking about you is enough to send me over the edge. Trust me."

"Really?" she asked with a wicked grin. "You have jacked off to me before?"

"Hundreds of times. If not thousands." I laughed. I could see she was confused by that admission. "Amanda, I don't think you quite understand how obsessed with you I was. You are incandescent. Strong. Passionate. And not to mention hot as hell."

"Even with this hair?" She rolled her eyes, pulling at a strand of her newly dark hair.

"Oh yes," I admitted. "You know, I used to think I had a thing for redheads because of you. Now, with this color," I ran my fingers through her locks, "I know I just had a thing for you."

"Had?" she challenged. "I'd say I still affect you." She wiped her lips and winked at me. "Okay. I suppose we can get on the road now. I'm sure you're anxious to get going."

I cocked my head. "Oh no," I said. "I'm not that guy."

"What guy?"

"The guy who gets off and doesn't reciprocate. Get your ass on that bed. It's my turn."

"Sweet Jesus," she panted but quickly complied.

As she moved to the bed, she pushed the bags I'd brought in with us to the ground. One of them tipped over, spilling out the contents. Some cash, a passport, and a set of cuffs came out.

"Cuffs?" she challenged.

I shrugged. "I like to be prepared for any situation."

Amanda taunted me then by bending over, showing off her glorious bare ass, and picking up the cuffs off the floor.

"You have a key for these?"

"In the bag, yes."

Amanda raised an eyebrow. "So, if I were to take one of these, and slip it on my wrist, like this..." She placed a cuff on her left hand.

"Amanda, what are you—"

"And if I were to cuff you to me to make sure you didn't leave," she whispered, holding up the other cuff.

"You seriously think I'd abandon you in your time of need," I asked. My voice was suddenly husky.

She shrugged. "Everyone else does."

"I'm not everyone else," I assured her, pushing her gently to sit on the bed. "You don't need to cuff me to you. I'm already attached." She giggled but spread her legs open wide.

"Prove it," she challenged.

God, she was beautiful. I slid the other cuff over the top of the bedpost. This way she could easily free herself, but the way she smirked, she enjoyed the fact I wanted her to stay exactly where she was. She licked her lips as I knelt between her thighs and dined on the most decadent dish I'd ever eaten in my life.

CHAPTER NINE

Connor

Malcolm and Amanda should be arriving any time now. Likely in the morning, as they would have needed time to sleep. Malcolm must have tied her up or something to prevent her from running. No way would she have gone with him willingly. She knew what I'd do to her if she did. Which meant Malcolm had to have taken her.

My teeth ground together, imagining him manhandling her. Granted I, too, had locked Amanda up to get her to obey me, but that was different. She was mine to command until she was sold. Malcolm didn't own Amanda. He'd stolen her. He would learn soon enough. No one stole from me.

I shifted on the rudimentary lookout Kenny had set up in the woods outside Malcolm's property. We were essentially perched in a tree like we were hunting deer or some shit. The structure felt stable enough given how quickly it was assembled.

"Jerky?" Kenny asked from his spot beside me. His breath reeked of tobacco and poor dental hygiene. He hadn't been hired for his appearance, but rather for his aim. He had his shot all lined up from the moment they arrived. Not that he'd need to take it. I'd told Kenny I wanted to give them time in the house. Give them a false sense of security and take them down when they were more relaxed.

That was only part of the reason. The other part was that I needed to see if Amanda was there willingly or if she'd been forced to join him. Her behavior around him would determine if she lived or died.

"Get your disgusting meat out of my face," I hissed, looking back at the cabin. Malcolm's surveillance system was proving to be tricky to navigate around. Even our position in the trees was farther away than I wanted. A clean shot from this distance wasn't a guarantee, but it was the closest we could get before we tripped off a sensor or ended up on camera.

"Your loss," Kenny said. He took a large bite out of the stick. We'd been up in this tree for hours now, and I was on edge. Kenny, however, seemed cool as a cucumber. He was a hunter. He was used to waiting for the prey to come to him.

Malcolm's escape plan was clever. I'd give him that. He left the same day I gave him to Amanda. Probably thought he'd have a two-week head start. Clearly, he didn't understand I guarded my property well. He was smart to have me remove her ankle monitor. But he'd quickly found the ones on her clothing. Not only that, he'd switched his ride. Twice that I knew of. The first switch had been easy enough to track. The second required my men to "negotiate" with the dealer to give up information on the VIN. When that car was spotted in a hotel, abandoned, I knew they'd switched cars for a third time. Bastard.

"Car," Kenny hissed, crouching low, gun positioned for my call.

"Wait," I whispered.

Together we hid in the shelter of the trees as a black SUV pulled into the driveway. The windows held the glare of the sun so neither of us could make out who was inside. The vehicle's engine turned off, but no one immediately got out. Just then the driver's side door opened and out stepped a large man with dark sunglasses. He was clean-shaven with wide shoulders. He was heavy around the middle which meant he might be a large guy, but he likely wasn't strong. A weakness. The man did, however, have a pistol in his hand.

"I have the shot," Kenny whispered beside me.

"That's not Malcolm, dipshit. Looks like a hired goon. Wait."

Kenny didn't move his weapon but continued to follow his movements through his scope.

The goon seemed to be surveying the area. Again. Smart. Exactly what I would have done. Send someone to check that the drop-off was clear before depositing the goods.

The man knelt on the ground, seeming to look for footprints.

"Did you leave prints?" I hissed.

"No boss. I didn't get that close. The sensors are a good hundred yards from the driveway. If he picks up anything, it won't be us."

"He better not."

The goon looked around as though searching for us. I held my breath. Not that I feared for my life. Kenny could take this guy out before he even lifted his gun, but if he died, so too did my chances of getting Amanda. If Malcolm didn't get confirmation the coast was clear, he wouldn't bring her here. And he couldn't get that confirmation if the suit was dead.

The guy then walked up to the house and tried the doors and windows, which triggered the alarms. He quickly used his phone, tapping a few times, and the alarms went off. Interesting. The goon had access to the house.

A moment later he made a call.

"Yeah. I'm here," he said to someone on the other end of the line. "No sign of anyone. Doors and windows triggered when I tried them. I've reset the system. Nothing's been here other than maybe a deer or two. You should be good."

The guy looked at his watch. "Will do." He hung up and put his cell in his suit pocket.

"Take him down, but I need him alive."

He smiled at me. "Will do."

Kenny aimed, and in one silent shot, hit the goon's right hand, knocking out his gun. It flew into the woods. Panic-stricken, the wounded man lunged for the car before a second shot took out his ankle.

"Kenny, enough. I can't leave a trail of blood on the driveway."

"Sorry."

I sighed. This would be a mess to clean up, and I didn't know how long I had to do it. "Cover me. If he goes for the phone, take out his other hand."

Kenny nodded as I climbed out of the tree. I wasn't worried about going onto the driveway now. The sensors would have already tripped that there was someone here. However, if the SUV lingered too long in the driveway, that might alert Malcolm that something was up. Which meant I needed to get him in the car and offsite quickly.

When I reached the bastard, he was trying to make a tourniquet for his hand with his tie. His ankle seemed to be a clean shot straight through, but it was still bleeding all over the gravel driveway.

"Give me your phone," I said. I wasn't worried about him trying to make a run for his gun. Not with that injury.

Pulling free my own weapon, I took deadly aim at his brain. It would be a mess to clean up, but if he budged, I wouldn't hesitate.

"I won't ask again." I nodded toward his breast pocket where I'd seen him put it.

"Fine. Jesus." The man did his best to retrieve the phone using his good hand. "Here's my fucking phone." He tossed it over to me and it landed near my feet.

I bent down to get it, keeping the gun on him the whole time. "Now get in the car."

"I can't walk, asshole. You shot me in the fucking foot."

"Want me to shoot you in the other one? Or how about a shot to the dick?"

The man's eyes bugged, so I lowered the gun to his crotch to prove I wasn't fucking around. Men could endure lots of pain, but mess around with their groin and they complied with ease.

Hobbling, the man got up as I hovered beside him, ready to

take him down if he made any attempt to escape. When he got to the back of the SUV, I opened the rear hatch.

"Get the fuck inside." I pulled out zip ties from my back pocket.

It took some work, but I got him in the cargo area and secured his good wrist to the metal hooks meant for car seats. Those fuckers came in handy.

Once he was secure, I uncocked my gun, slid it into the back of my pants, and opened the side door.

Working as fast as possible, I scooped up as much of the bloody gravel as I could and dumped it straight into the car. Once most of it was inside, I scuffed up the rest of the gravel to hide the evidence before I hopped into the driver's seat, turned the ignition, and backed out of the driveway.

Checking the rearview mirror, I saw my prisoner was still writhing in pain. Good. Right where I wanted him. It was time to have a little chat about the security setup of Malcolm's safehouse.

AMANDA

"I swear, there was a key in the bag the last time I used them," Malcolm said frantically. He searched the pile on the bed that he'd dumped out to hunt for the key. This was his third attempt at trying to find it.

"Who was the lucky gal who got to use them last time?" I took the other cuff off the bedpost. I tried to come off coy, but instead, it came out horribly jealous. Which I was.

"Well, *he* didn't like being in the cuffs quite as much as you did. Some punk-ass thief who tried to steal one of my paintings. One of my actual paintings. Ironic, yes, I know. Relax, I didn't hurt him. I didn't even turn him in. I just held him long enough to determine if he'd been hired by someone else to spy on my operations. Turns out he was just a punk kid who thought he had sticky fingers and could make a few bucks selling one of my pieces on eBay!" Malcolm shook his head.

"What was his name?"

"Hell if I remember. Something with an H, I think. Probably made up. Not the point. The point is he thought he could steal art. From me. The nerve."

"Now you know how Connor feels." I flinched realizing my comment brought our reality crashing back down on us.

"So...how do we get these off me?" I wanted to change the subject.

Malcolm rubbed his hands over his face. "We don't. Not until we get to the cabin. I keep a few sets there too. One of them is bound to have a key that works. If not, I have bolt cutters."

"Fun."

"We'll be there soon. Can you tolerate having it on your wrist until then?"

"I don't see another choice, but yes, I can handle a heavy bracelet. God knows I've endured worse than this."

Malcolm came up to me then and pulled me into his arms, causing me to shrink. At first, the move was so sudden. When he placed his lips on my head, my muscles relaxed. I leaned into the embrace. "I'm sorry. This will be over soon. I promise."

"I know." I didn't doubt it would be over soon. I just thought Malcolm and I had different ideas of what "over" meant. Sure, Malcolm would keep me safe up until Connor found us. After that, all bets were off.

"Can I have a few minutes in the bathroom before we leave? I could use a shower, assuming it's okay to get these wet?"

"Yeah, it's fine. They're rust-proof. I have some calls to make. We'll leave as soon as you're done."

Part of me was hoping Malcolm would join me in the shower, but he was far too practical for that. He was on a mission, and I'd distracted him long enough.

After the world's fastest shower, I came out of the bathroom with just a towel around my torso. My dark hair was still dripping some of the black dye. The housekeeping staff were going to love me.

"Leave the towel. I got us a new ride." He tossed me my clothes, indicating I needed to hurry.

Once I was dressed and we checked out, I started to head for the Jetta, but he pulled my hand in another direction. He was taking us to the convenience store across the street.

"More provisions? Or are you just tired of Doritos for breakfast?"

"Grab a few things for the road, but we're not going back to the car. We're hopping on that bus." He pointed to a large gray bus parked alongside the store.

"What? I thought we couldn't..." I whispered.

"I'm getting tired. I need the rest. I want to be sharp when we arrive at the safehouse. We both need the sleep." He looked over his shoulder. "My contact says the house is secure. By taking the bus we can be there by morning. They don't seem to be set up for cameras, so we should be okay. I'll pay cash. Just keep your hat pulled low."

Thirty minutes later, we were on the road, a bag of food shoved into the two duffle bags, and safely tucked into the back seats of the bus. Malcolm took the window seat because he didn't want my face to be seen by anyone on the outside.

One look at him and you could tell he was weary. The dark circles under his eyes betrayed how tired he was. I could relate. The last days were starting to take a toll. He was right. We both needed the rest.

To help encourage him to close his eyes, I placed my head on his shoulder and nuzzled against him to get comfortable. He reached out to take my cuffed hand. He quickly placed his suit jacket over them to hide the cuffs.

"Don't let go of my hand, okay?" Malcolm whispered. "If I'm going to sleep, I need to know you're right here."

I responded by squeezing his hand. That must have done the

trick because a moment later, I heard him softly sawing logs. I followed shortly after him.

I'd never been much of a dreamer, always envying people who had vivid dreams at night. I never did. I went to sleep and then woke up. Almost like a pause button had been hit. So when I saw Connor's face hovered over mine, I struggled to know if it was real or a nightmare.

"There you are," he whispered against my ear. "I've been searching for you."

"Connor?"

"It's me, baby. We can finally be together. You can be my pet, and I will protect you, forever and always. Just like you wanted."

"How did you find me?"

"I never lost you. I was just waiting for him to screw up. And he did. Now I'm here. You don't have to be scared anymore.

Connor leaned close and pressed his lips against mine. I wanted to scream, but I knew that if I did, I was as good as gone.

"I knew I'd find you."

Connor's breath was hot against my neck. I could feel his fingers wrapping around my neck, ready to squeeze the life out of me if I said the wrong thing.

"I've been so scared. I missed you so much, Connor."

The lies came so easily.

"You don't need to be afraid anymore. I took care of him."

Fear sank into my pores.

"What? How?" Those were the only words I could get out.

"He won't bother you anymore." Connor reached into his suit jacket pocket and pulled out Malcolm's severed dick.

I woke with a start.

"You okay?" Malcolm said beside me. The sun was up and the bus was still moving. My eyes darted down to his pants. There was no blood. His member was still intact. I let loose a huge sigh of relief.

"Bad dream," I said. Rubbing the sleep from my eyes, I tried to slow down the beating of my heart. Being with Malcolm, it was so easy to forget the very real danger that I was in should Connor or his thugs find us.

"You're safe. Okay? He's not going to find you."

"How do you know I was dreaming about that?"

Malcolm stared out the window, jaw tensed. "You talk in your sleep."

"I do?"

"You do. We're here." He stood up as the bus pulled into a small gas station. "There should be a car waiting for us." He started walking to the front of the bus as it came to a stop. "A few more minutes and this will all be over."

Over. Right. Somehow, I didn't believe that.

CHAPTER TEN

Connor

According to the "No Trespassing" sign where I moved the SUV, the area was closed off to hunters for the season. Perfect. No one should be in the woods. That was the beauty of rural communities. Things were so spread out. It was easy to hide among the trees. No one would be around to hear his screams. And scream he would.

Opening the hatch, I smiled as the injured man did his best to scoot away from me. Hard to do when you were hog-tied to the vehicle, but his attempt was valiant. There was no escaping what was about to happen.

I rolled my neck slowly from side to side to let my captive know in no uncertain terms that I was in no rush. Even though I was. It was better to let them think you had all the time in the world to get what you wanted. When he looked properly terrified, I spoke.

"I'll ask you this question once before you regret not answering me the first time," I said. "What's your name and who do you work for?"

"Fuck you."

"Good. We get to do this the fun way." I searched the wooded surroundings until I found what I wanted. A fallen branch about the size of a baseball bat.

Without warning, I started swinging at the broken man. First to the injured ankle, then the chest. I resisted going for the head. I didn't want him dead, yet. I still needed information.

"Hodge!" he yelled after the sixth blow. "My name is Hodge."

"There. That wasn't so hard. Now, Hodge, who do you work for?"

"No one. I'm an independent contractor," Hodge said. He was struggling to catch his breath. The way he hunched to the side; I suspected I had broken one of his ribs. I'd break a whole lot more than that if he didn't start talking.

"Well, Mr. Independent Contractor, why were you inspecting that house?"

"I was hired to check on the property."

I lifted the branch in warning. "Hired by *who*?"

"I don't know his name," Hodge said, though it was clear he was lying.

I was done playing this game. I tossed the branch to the ground. Hodge was going to need harsher encouragement to talk, apparently. Fine. I could do harsh.

Reaching into my pocket, I pulled out a cigar cutter. The very one that removed Gwen's finger so efficiently. I held it up and gave it a quick pinch to showcase the blade in action. The sounds of the blade slicing the air made Hodge's eyes bulge.

"Did you know these are excellent at removing fingers?"

Hodge curled his bloodied fingers into a fist to try and protect them from me.

"I wonder...what else might it slice through?" I glanced down at his pants. "No. I don't swing that way, so your cock is safe. For now. Hmmm, but what else might we take off?"

Hodge screamed for help, but I wasn't worried. Slowly I climbed into the back with him. "Ah. I know." I held his neck against the seat with my left hand and quickly slid the cutter over the tip of his nose with my right. Hodge's eyes widened as sweat poured down his face. "I bet this would work. What do you think?"

Hodge squirmed under me but quickly started singing like a canary.

"Luxx. Fucking Malcolm Luxx. Alright? He hired me. It's his house."

"Thank you for your confirmation of what I already knew." Then, without warning, I sliced the top of his nose clean off. Through his screams, I climbed back out of the SUV. "I did warn you that you would regret not answering my questions the first time I asked."

Hodge writhed in pain. I scanned my surroundings to confirm we were still hidden. Kenny was around somewhere, but I had no way of knowing if my back was covered or not.

"Now. What time is Malcolm arriving at the house?" Hodge was bleeding all over the car. I'd have to torch the vehicle anyway. Far too much DNA inside. But that was a problem for later. I needed information and I needed it fast.

"Tomorrow morning," Hodge grunted. "I don't know what time. He didn't give me specifics. He never gives specifics."

Smart.

"Are you supposed to make contact with him again?"

I could see the fear and the anger behind Hodge's eyes. I held up the cigar cutter. He didn't want to tell me shit, but he also didn't want to see what else I might cut off.

"I'm supposed to wait at the edge of the drive," Hodge finally said. "Flash my lights if the coast is clear. If I don't... If I'm not there, he'll keep driving."

Shit. That meant I had to keep him alive, at least until morning. Fine. I pulled out Hodge's phone and wiggled it in front of him.

"You want to live to see tomorrow? Then I need access to that safehouse. Now."

"He's got cameras, dipshit," Hodge sputtered. "You think you can just waltz up to his door and get inside? Password or not? He'll get you on camera. Hell, he's probably already watched you take me down. He's likely en route to another safehouse. The man evades police for a living, and you think you can pull up with two shooters and outsmart him?"

I flinched. Fuck. I hadn't even thought about driveway cameras.

"Try a dozen, asshole," I snapped, even though the rest of the team wouldn't be here until the next afternoon at the earliest.

Digging for my cell, I called Kenny.

"Camera situation. Can you take any of it down without looking suspicious?"

"He'd probably notice a bullet hole, huh?"

I pinched the edge of my nose. "Yeah, Kenny. I think he'd fucking notice that."

"Give me a few. I might have an idea."

Kenny hung up while I tried to weigh my options.

One, I might have a security breach with camera footage. If Malcolm had access to that footage, they might already have altered their course.

Two, it would take at least a few hours to re-scramble my men, but this time I'd have no leads on which direction they would have scattered to.

Three, I still had Hodge and his phone. There might be more information to gather inside the house.

Four, presuming Malcolm didn't see the footage, I could kill Hodge. Then take down Malcolm the second they got close enough to the driveway.

Fuck. None of this was going to plan.

My cell buzzed. It was Kenny.

"What did you figure out?" I hissed.

"I think I can take the transformer out. If I take that out, the footage would probably be lost once the generator went. But once that goes, then it's just manual locks. He'd be vulnerable."

"Do it. But make it look like it was an act of God."

"Huh?"

I pinched my eyebrows together in annoyance. "Get the chainsaw. Bring a tree down on the transformer. Make it look like an accident. He's no good in a vulnerable house if he doesn't stay in it. If he thinks we fucked with it, he'll ghost. Our only shot here is that he doesn't notice until it's too late to leave."

"Oh. Right. Yeah. Smart thinking. I'll go grab it."

While it might be crude, chainsaws were essential to the work my men did. They did the trick on bone and made disposal in garbage bags much more efficient.

I ended the call and leaned back against the back seat of the SUV. Hodge was rapidly losing blood. I honestly wasn't sure he'd survive the night.

"What can you tell me about Malcolm?" I asked. "Is he the sort of man who would kidnap a woman?"

"Fuck if I know. I check on his place a few times a year. He wires me a ton of money. That's all I know about the man."

"That's a pity. Because if you can't give me anything, what do I need you alive for?" I pulled out my gun and brought it to his head.

"You need me to flash those lights tomorrow," Hodge stuttered, the last pleadings of a dead man walking.

"Do I though? I just need your body and a pair of sunglasses. I can flash the lights from the floorboards." I cocked the gun.

"I...I...I can tell you about the house!" Hodge shouted.

Smiling, I lowered my weapon.

"I'm listening."

"Inside, it's basically a box. Two exits. One at the front of the house. The other's off the living room on the right. That leads to the power grid. From what I can gather, it's solar-powered. I haven't been on the roof, but I'd wager he's got some panels up there."

"Describe the layout."

Hodge shifted his weight, wincing against his injuries, but complied. "The main entrance brings you into a living room. There's a fireplace to your left as you come in. The bedroom is just past the living room, also on the left. The back right holds the kitchen and a walk-in pantry. It's fully stocked. The bathroom is to the right of the entrance. That's it. No basement. No upstairs."

"So we bust down a door or climb in through a window. Then there is nowhere for him to hide," I said, pondering my attack.

"It won't be that easy. The house has no windows. Not a one. And don't let the outside façade fool you. It's not drywall holding that house. It's concrete, And those two red entry doors? If you knock out the power, it won't matter. Those aren't normal doors. They're bank vault doors. Which you can't pick. I don't care how good you think you are. The only way you get in there is with my help."

"Do I though? Thank you for your cooperation," I said. Lifting the gun, I put a bullet clean through his right eye. I had what I needed from him. All he was now was a liability. And I never let liabilities live. Which was why Amanda better not become one.

MALCOLM

I knew it was childish of me to get jealous of her saying that she was thinking about Connor in her sleep, but still, it rattled me. Maybe she *did* have feelings for him and secretly wanted to go back. If she told me as much, would I let her go?

I shook my head. I'd have to. If that's what she wanted. Otherwise, I was no better than him.

"We're over here," I said, hoisting the bags over my shoulder as she got off the bus.

"Okay." She yawned as she followed after me.

Parked in the lot was the brand new truck Camila had set for us. Gassed up and ready to keep us on the road if we got to the safehouse and didn't get the all-clear. I put the bags down by the back tire and pretended to tie my shoe as I reached under the hub of the tire to get the key left for me.

I pressed the key fob and unlocked the doors. "Hop in."

She nodded her head but got in the back instead of the passenger's side. I raised an eyebrow.

"Safer this way," she said.

Nodding, I put the bags in the truck bed and then got into the driver's seat. I looked back and saw she had lain down in the back. She yawned again.

"You okay?" It was hard to believe she was still tired after sleeping on the bus, but maybe her sleep was as restless as mine had been.

"I'm okay. But I have decided that you were right."

"About?"

"I shouldn't know where we're going. It's safer for everyone if I don't. So I took one of the roofies you had stashed in the bag." She gave me a tired smile.

"You didn't..."

She nodded and closed her eyes. "Nighty night."

Well shit. Guess I had about an hour to get to the safehouse before she woke up. Stubborn fool. I shook my head and put my seatbelt on. At least she could see the logic behind it, but now that she was drifting off, I couldn't help but feel a level of pride that she trusted me enough to be unconscious around me. That had to say something about how she felt for me. Right?

While she settled in for her "nap," I started the truck and got on the road. I called Camila for an update.

"Thanks for the ride. Anything to report?" I asked as soon as she picked up.

"You're alive. That's good," she said. "All is quiet on our end, which makes me nervous as fuck. Anything happening there?"

I scanned in both directions before I turned onto the road that would bring us to the house. Soon, she'd be safe, and I'd have a moment to think about how to bring this bastard down.

"I heard from Hodge," I said. "Things look good on his end. He'll give me an all-clear before we head in though. Once we're settled, I'll call on a different burner just to let you know we made it. Then I want you and Darcy to disappear for a while. Like deep shadow. Okay? I don't want you on his radar."

My mind flashed back to that woman losing her pinky. I had to fight back the bile.

"You don't have to tell me twice. We're already on the road. Your affairs are in order for three months."

"Thank you, Camila."

"You just make sure you invite us to the wedding, okay?"

"Wedding? We're not—"

"No, but you will be," Camila said confidently. "One day. She's the *one*, Malcolm. You'd have to be blind not to see that. Darcy even sees it, and she never picked up on me drooling over her all those years ago. Now go, get your girl locked up, and then maybe you can get her knocked up." She chuckled.

I rolled my eyes. "Goodbye, Camila."

I hung up to the sounds of her laughter. I was glad she was able to laugh, even if it was at my expense. After everything I'd put them through in the last few days, I'd happily take the jabs.

In about thirty minutes, we'd be inside the safehouse and maybe then I could take a breath. The tension in my shoulders was nearly unbearable.

If Hodge wasn't there to wave us in, I'd keep driving and take us to the Florida house. It would mean more time on the road, but I wasn't risking her safety.

Climbing up the last hill, I heard Amanda's soft snores coming from the back. The sound made me relax. Soon, we'd reach our destination. Or we'd be starting our second leg. It would all depend on one flash of headlights.

CHAPTER ELEVEN

Connor

Once I'd managed to get myself cleaned up from the mess Hodge had left on me, I backed the SUV out of the woods and waited on the side of the road, ready to flash the headlights at Malcolm, and prayed he wouldn't look too closely at the figure in the driver's seat.

Hodge and I had only our skin color in common. He was easily a hundred pounds heavier than me, bald, and clean-shaven. I had dark sunglasses to hide my eyes, and there was a baseball cap of Hodge's sitting on the driver's seat. Perfect. That would disguise a lot of the differences. All except one big one. I reached into my back pocket and called Kenny.

"You wouldn't happen to have a razor with you by chance?"

"A razor? Um. No. But I got me a bait knife. That's sharp enough to take the scales off a fish. What do you need to cut?"

I sighed. "My beard. I need to become Hodge from a distance."

"Who is Hodge?"

"The guy you shot. And the one I just killed. Turns out he is supposed to flash them the all-clear from the SUV when they get here."

"Ah. Well, this should work then."

"I'm going to need any extra clothes you may have too. I need to look heavier."

"Yeah, I got me a bulky camo jacket that you could put under something.'"

"Perfect. I'm on my way to you. Don't shoot me."

Kenny laughed. "You got it, boss."

While it wasn't the cleanest shave I'd ever had, the gutting knife had done a surprisingly decent job of removing the hair to better match Hodge's appearance.

Looking at my bare face in the rearview mirror, I smiled. I didn't look the same. I didn't necessarily look like Hodge either, but from far away, with his suit jacket over Kenny's hunting gear, it might just be enough. I highly doubted Malcolm would stop and ask me to get out of the car. He'd be too focused on getting his stolen merchandise safe. All he'd be looking for was the vehicle and the signal.

And if he *did* approach the car, then I'd be ready for him. My pistol was within reach. Either way, this fucker was going to end up with a bullet in his brain. If I had to sacrifice intelligence on what he knew about my business before he died, so be it. But at the end of this, he'd be joining Hodge when we burnt the rig to a crisp. And depending on how Amanda reacted to seeing me, there might be a third body to destroy.

Once I was happy with my disguise, I slumped in the seat as Hodge was a few inches shorter than me. I was as ready as I was going to be.

I needed to see, with my own eyes, how they interacted when they thought no one was watching them. If they walked into that place hand in hand, then I'd know I'd been played. If she was kicking and screaming, well then, Malcolm alone would die. Painfully.

Just then, I saw headlights appear at the top of the hill. I reached for my cell. This was a quiet road. I'd only seen a handful of cars since Kenny and I arrived. And none of them had been brand new trucks.

Calling Kenny, I put him on speakerphone. "Eyes sharp. I think he's here. Wait for my order."

"You got it, Boss."

As the truck got closer to the driveway, it slowed. It didn't put on a blinker but rather just came close, as though waiting for a signal. Hodge's signal.

I flashed my headlights and kept my eyes as low as I could. For a moment, the truck didn't do anything. But then, after a painful second, it turned up the driveway. I let loose a breath.

"They're on their way up the drive," I said. I got out of the SUV as quietly as I could. Then I ran through the woods, trying to catch up to the truck so I could see what was going on. It was difficult in the dense forest not to make noise while jumping over fallen trees or roots. Granted, I had Kenny as my eyes, but he wasn't going to take the shot without my say, so I had to haul ass to get through the woods.

That's when I heard the sound of a door closing and cursed under my breath. I was still too far away to see their interaction. Moving as quickly as I could, I listened intently. Footsteps on gravel. The jingle of keys.

Move faster, Connor!

As I approached the top of the hill, I saw that the front door of the cabin was open. Malcolm was just inside the door. In each hand, he held two large duffle bags that he placed inside. But no Amanda. Had he chopped her up and put her in those bags? My stomach lurched.

That's when I saw Malcolm come back out of the cabin. His eyes were darting around, so I had to crouch down low to be hidden.

He was on edge. Like he was ready to bolt. After a moment, he let free a breath and went to the passenger's side of the truck. He opened the back seat cab and pulled out Amanda. My heart stopped. Her once red hair was now jet black, but her face was plain as day. I'd know those lips anywhere.

She didn't seem to be conscious, but she was breathing. I could see her chest rise and fall. Malcolm picked her up and tossed her over his right shoulder like she was a sack of potatoes. Her ass was in the air, her arms dangled limp down his back. He must have drugged her. I knew that ragdoll position well. It's how all my pets used to come to me before I had the kennel set up. Now they walked right into their cages. Cut my expenses dramatically.

That's when I caught the glint of something in the sunlight. Something shiny and metallic as he climbed up the stairs with her lifeless body. Dangling from her left hand was a handcuff.

My blood boiled.

This was the confirmation I needed. She hadn't left with him of her own free will. Malcolm had taken my property by force. He'd kidnapped my kidnap.

I'd seen enough.

"Take Malcolm down. *Just* Malcolm," I whispered into the cell.

AMANDA

I didn't know how long I'd been out, but when I finally came to, I was on the floor. It was cold and dark. My eyes were having a hard time adjusting to the dim lighting while my brain struggled to push free of the fog the roofie had placed me under.

Where was I?

One thing was certain, I was no longer in the truck, and this sure as shit didn't feel like a cabin in the woods. I reached out a hand and felt the wall beside me. It was metal, smooth, cold. Like a cage.

A chill ran over me.

Connor. He must have found us. And now I was trapped again. Scrambling up to my feet, I could feel my heart thrumming wildly as I tried to reconcile what was happening. My body tensed as I took in the size of the room. It was about the width and length of a car. Maybe twelve feet by twenty-four? That's when I realized I was standing on a thin camping mattress. I was surprised to find that Connor had left me a blanket and pillow.

There were no windows. Only a dim glow on the other side of the room. Carefully, I approached the light holding my breath. As I got closer, I discovered what the glow was. Computer screens. Lots of them. Seven in total. Each screen showed nothing but static.

What the hell was going on?

That's when I saw the door. I knew it would be locked before I even tried it, but try it I did.

"Fuck," I cursed. My voice echoed loudly against the metal walls. Something told me this cage was soundproof as well.

My next thought dropped me to my knees. If Connor had me caged, where was Malcolm? My stomach sank. I already knew the answer to that. If Connor found us, that would mean Malcolm was dead. Connor wouldn't have allowed him to live. I blanched, thinking of the ways he might have been tortured before finally being taken down. I knew firsthand what the monster was capable of. I had no doubt my fate would follow in Malcolm's footsteps.

As I curled myself into a ball against the cold wall, I stared at the locked door and felt myself come to terms with my reality. There were no tears. There was no point. Tears never helped. They wouldn't change my situation or bring Malcolm back. All there was to do was sit and wait for Connor to open the door to kill me. It would be a welcome end.

CHAPTER TWELVE

CONNOR

My order was clear: Take Malcolm down. And yet...there was no shot fired. I stood and watched in disbelief as Malcolm walked into his fortress with *my* pet over his shoulder. I stood there, helpless, as the door locked behind them.

"Kenny!" I hissed into the phone. The screen, however, was black. I pushed the power button but got nothing. The battery must have died. "Fuck."

Racing back up to the tree Kenny had perched in, I found him there, gun still at the ready.

He looked over at me.

"Why didn't you take the fucking shot?"

"You didn't give the order."

I ground my teeth together. "I did, but my fucking phone must have died. I need yours."

"It's about as useful as yours. I only got one bar if I'm lucky. I was amazed you were able to text me at all out here, honestly."

I held up his phone and sure enough, it was barely registering a bar. I was about to ask him if he had a charger, but the dickhead had an ancient-as-fuck model phone. Even if he had one, it wouldn't work on my phone.

"Next shot you have of Malcolm, take it," I said. I gave him back his phone. "Leave the girl alive. Understood?"

Kenny nodded, then went back to watching the house.

"Where did you end up parking your car after you dropped me here?"

"About three miles south. Why?"

"I need to get a new phone or a charger at the very least and check on my reinforcements. Now that he's locked inside, he won't be going anywhere. He'll hunker down. Which means I need to change tactics. This asshole is going down. Even if I have to burn his ass out."

"Why not take the SUV that the bald dude had?"

"You mean the one that's a literal crime scene and is holding a dead body? That one? You want me to drive that one in town and hope Hodge's blood isn't dripping out the back?"

"Ah. Right. Well, I guess you can use mine. Parked it on the edge of town at a hiking spot. Follow the main road. You'll find it eventually. Oh, and don't mind the *Playboy* in the front seat. A man has needs."

I knew all about the needs of a man. I'd made my fortune on it. Kenny had never wanted a pet though. He didn't have the means to care for one, as he was always on the go for me and others who hired his skillset. The one downside of pet ownership was: it took a lot of work. Realistically, it wasn't a thing most men could maintain. Which was why my clients were wealthy. They had the means to keep the pets monitored and cared for offsite while they lived their double lives. Family man on the weekdays and then, on the weekends while "golfing," they'd get their freak on with their pets who were holed up in a nice undisclosed hiding spot. No one was the wiser.

"I'll do my best not to jack off in your truck," I muttered, taking the keys he held out for me.

"Dude. Not cool. Now I have that image in my head."

"I'll be back as soon as I can. Keep an eye out. If he steps a toe outside, shoot that fucking toe off, then kill the bastard."

"And the woman? Want her wounded so she can't run?"

My body reacted without thinking. My hand wrapped around his throat and was squeezing before I could even stop it. "Don't touch her. She's *mine*. Understood? Mine."

Kenny's eyes bugged, but he nodded. I choked him a moment longer before I let him go.

It was the second time I'd shown my hand to Kenny. He knew that Amanda was important to me. Which was now leverage against me. When all of this was done and Amanda was safe and back under my protection, Kenny would have to die. No one could know my weakness. It was a pity. Sharpshooters were hard to find.

Shrugging free of the bloody hunter's jacket Kenny had given me, I did my best to clean the rest of Hodge's blood off me before I walked into town. I couldn't very well get stopped by the cops and be taken in for questioning as to why I was caked in blood. Not that I was worried about jail time. I had the funds to bribe a judge, but I didn't have the luxury of time to waste on stupid mistakes.

Fuck Malcolm and the hurdles he was making me jump through to get Amanda back. Besides the outright theft of my property, he was now encroaching on my business affairs. I shouldn't be away from my kennel for this long. Anita was only given instructions to feed the pets for a few days. Highly stupid on my part. I needed to get back immediately.

I'd get Kenny's truck, buy a new charger, and contact my reinforcements. Then I'd call Vincent to see if he could get an intermediary in to check on my pets and take care of Anita if she decided to grow a conscience.

But first, I had the three-mile walk through East Bum-Fuck while trying not to get eaten alive by these damn persistent tiny black flies. After I killed Malcolm, I was going to leave his body in the woods for those fuckers to suck his blood dry. Asshole.

MALCOLM

I was on edge. Even though we were safely tucked into the cabin, I didn't feel the ease I thought I would. Instead, I couldn't shake the sense we were being watched.

I needed to check the perimeter. But because Amanda was still conked out from the roofie, I didn't feel safe leaving her inside and helpless should there be an ambush waiting for me outside. Out of an abundance of caution, I put her in the panic room. Yes, it was a bit excessive to have a panic room inside of a safehouse, but I was a paranoid person.

Laying her down on the bed and covering her with a blanket, I locked her in. I left a note by her pillow letting her know what I'd done so she wouldn't panic if she woke up in another cage. That was the last thing I wanted.

Satisfied that she would be safe while I checked the grounds, I made my way to the front door. The frame had a small peephole on the side of the doorway. From the outside, the peephole looked like a knot in the wood. Traditional peepholes were positioned too high so you wouldn't catch people crouching below. Mine were positioned at waist level. Like I said. Paranoid.

There didn't seem to be anyone outside. I pondered and checked again. Moving to the back door, I did the same visual checks, but kept the doors shut, just in case. While nothing seemed off, the uneasy feeling wouldn't go away.

With the doors securely locked, I checked on our provisions in the house. The girls had done an excellent job of keeping the properties operational. We had bedsheets, blankets, bath towels, toilet paper, and plenty of non-perishables. We'd be good here for at least three months. It should be enough time for things to cool off and to figure out a plan. Seeing all of this should have made me feel at ease. But I wasn't.

Opting to check the outdoor camera footage of Hodge's inspection, I headed back to the panic room where the tapes were. I could see if there were any gaps in his surveillance.

The entrance to the panic room was in the kitchen. It had been built behind a false wall in the pantry. Granted, it was excessive, but so were the shady practices in the black market. I'd spent a good week in that room when a job went south a few years ago. I might have accidentally stolen art from a mob boss. There was a price on the head of whoever did it. Fortunately, no one knew that it was me, and when the painting turned up in an alley garbage bin, undamaged, the hunt to find the thief ended. Still, I'd stayed the week. Men and their toys were unpredictable.

Opening the door as quietly as I could to not disturb Amanda's sleep, I was greeted instead, not by her soft snores, but by absolute silence.

For a moment, I panicked when I didn't see her head on the pillow. But then I saw her curled up in the corner. Her arms were wrapped tight around her knees. Her eyes were open, but she was not seeing anything. It was like her spirit had left her body and she was just a shell.

"Amanda?" She didn't move or even respond to the sound of my voice. "Amanda, look at me." I knelt beside her. She made no attempt to move or even blink. "Amanda? What is it? What's wrong?"

I looked around to see if she'd been hurt, or maybe bitten by a snake or something, but then it hit me. She'd woken up alone on a mattress on the floor. She was in a box. A locked box. She thought she'd been captured again. She didn't see my note. I cursed.

Lifting her in my arms, I brought her out of the panic room and into the living room. While the living room was brighter, there were no windows to let in any sun. It was just the artificial glow of the overhead lights that illuminated the room. And even then, they cast hard shadows on everything.

Sitting down with her still in my arms on the leather sofa, I tried to get her out of the state of self-preservation she'd thrown herself into.

"Amanda, look at me, please. You're safe. You're with Malcolm. Connor isn't here. You were in my panic room while I checked the house. I'm so sorry. Amanda, please be okay." I felt tears stinging my eyes wondering just how much damage I'd done to her psyche.

Over and over, I whispered her name softly against her head until I felt a small movement from her hand. It twitched a few times, then she slowly reached up, grabbed onto my shirt, and hung on to me for dear life. I pulled her closer to me and held her there in my arms until we both fell asleep.

When I awoke, it was to the feel of something warm on my neck. At first, I thought it was Amanda's breathing, but it was wet. Cracking an eye open, I saw her straddled on top of me. Her shirt was off, leaving her bare breasts right in front of my line of vision.

"Are we safe?" she whispered.

I nodded, still too stunned to speak.

"No sign of Connor?"

I shook my head this time.

"Good. So we can finally do this." She lowered her lips to mine.

The moan I let loose was deep and uncontrolled. This woman did something to me that many had tried but failed to stir in me. I wanted her. And she knew it.

My hands gripped her hips. My thumbs traced the edges of her panties, which was the only barrier she'd left on.

"Amanda. No. We can't do this," I managed between her kisses.

"Malcolm, please," she whispered. "I need you. I need you inside of me. Please." She lowered her hands to my pants, but I stopped her before she could get any further.

"Why? Why do you need this?" She blinked at me. "Do you think I'm owed something for getting you to safety, or are you using sex as a way to escape the reality you're faced with again?" Neither answer would be right, of course. Hell, it might have been a cruel question, but one I deserved to know the answer to.

Amanda withdrew her hands fully and sat back to look at me with disappointment. Her silence spoke volumes. She didn't want sex. Not with me.

CHAPTER THIRTEEN

Amanda

Sitting straddled across his lap, bare-breasted and rejected, I wondered if Malcolm might be right. Were my actions to try and have sex with him a trauma response? After all, I had been through a shit storm of it the last few days. If I stopped to process everything I'd been through, my head might explode. Was this how I was avoiding my feelings? By throwing myself at Malcolm? To feel something other than the abject fear lying just beneath the surface?

Sex had always protected me from pain by cruel men in the past. It had been my one "get out of jail free" move. Is that what I was doing to Malcolm? Was I trying to ensure my safety by sleeping with him? I didn't want to think so, but now he had me second-guessing myself. I was utterly confused. He was the first man to ever push my advances away.

Part of me was stung that he wasn't instantly taking me up on my offer of sex. And I probably would have gotten up and run away from the embarrassment of the rejection if I hadn't noticed his hands were still locked onto my hips. He was giving me an out, but he also didn't want to let me go. He was conflicted. As was I.

I studied his eyes trying to make sense of the question he'd asked. I realized what he was asking: In what way would I be using him?

"You don't have to answer me." Malcolm sighed. His fingers released my hips, and I hated how the small retreat felt.

"So," I snapped, "the only reason I might want to have sex with you is either as a thank you or as an escape from reality. Those are the only two options?"

He shrugged and looked away from me. That was exactly what he thought. He wasn't rejecting me, but himself. He didn't think he was worthy of my desire.

"Hey, look at me," I said. Reluctantly, he brought his dark eyes up to mine. I cupped his face in my hands. The stubble of his five o'clock shadow prickled against my fingers. "The reason I want to have sex with you is because I want to. Okay?"

"Just like you wanted to with Connor?"

His words took the wind out of me. Worse than a slap to the face. That was a hit to the heart.

"I'm sorry. That was mean," he said quickly. "That was pure jealousy talking. I shouldn't have said that."

I forced myself off his lap then picked up my shirt and put it back on. I sat in the chair opposite him and pulled my knees to my chest.

"Amanda, please. I'm sorry. I—"

"No. It's a valid question." Turning my body to face him, I gave him a small smile. "Yes, I had sex with Connor. A lot of it. And yes, part of that was probably survival instincts. My whole life I've been taught that it's better to submit to a man, especially an angry one, than to try and run. They always overpower you if you try. So sure, my body likely took it upon itself to give into him so that I could live to see another day." Malcolm's face contorted in pain. "*But* I won't lie. Part of me that enjoyed the fact that Connor, as demented as he was, was in many ways like me. Twisted. Broken. Disposable. There was a recognition of shared trauma in his eyes that I understood. As cruel as he was to me and the others, some small part of me got why he was doing it. If you never got love as a kid, it would make sense that when you became an adult, you would find a way to steal it...

"The point is, with Connor, I guess I saw fragments of the man he could have been if his life had turned out differently. If he had been nurtured instead of tortured as a child. And in those flashes, he was tender with me. Affectionate. Hell, even protective. The way he looked at me in those moments...it was new for me."

"Amanda, I wasn't trying to imply—"

"I liked fucking Connor. I won't deny it. I get how twisted that makes me. How broken and unlovable. Trust me, I get it. And deep down, that part of me makes you sick. You hate that a monster like him could ever turn me on. Trust me, I hate it too, but it doesn't change the truth of it."

Malcolm's hands dug through his hair as he lowered his head. "I'm not Connor, Amanda. I never will be. If you love him, I'm not judging you but, if you do. Then—"

"I don't love him," I said simply. Malcolm didn't look convinced. "Being sexually aroused by someone isn't the same thing as being in love with them. Sure, I was confused by how he made me feel. I know that it wasn't love...but it was *something*. Which, for me, was new," I admitted. "Here's the thing, Malcolm, the men in my life have always wanted me for what I could give them. One failed relationship after another. They get what they want from me then move on to the next model. I was worth only what my body could give them. Hell, that's why I was taken in the first place! So I could tend to the sexual deviancy of other men." I got up and started to pace around the small living room.

"And then you get dragged into this mess that is my life," I continued. "And what do you do? Instead of taking me as a pet and making me do your bidding, as I assumed you would do, you set me free. You put your career at risk and your life on the line to make sure I was safe. And you never once, not once, asked me for a sexual favor in return."

"Amanda, I told you, that has never been my intention."

"I know." I smiled. "And that's what you don't understand. That is a first for me. I've never had a guy check in with me so much to make sure a kiss or a touch was okay. And I sure as shit have never needed to justify why I wanted to have sex with someone."

"I never want you to do anything you don't want to do."

"I know. What I don't get is why?" I challenged.

The question seemed to take him off guard. "Because I respect you too much."

Frowning, I walked over to him and re-straddled him. He sucked in a breath. "Why do you respect me?"

He swallowed hard.

"It's because you love me, isn't it?"

There was no hesitation as he nodded. "Since high school."

I leaned down and pressed my lips gently to his. "And that's the reason I want to be with you. I don't want to have sex with you, Malcolm. I want to make love to you. That would be a first for me."

"Wait, are you saying that you love—"

"I don't know what I'm saying. I mean, we've only just re-connected. Did I have an insane crush on you in high school? Yes. But I don't know fully the man you've grown into." I reached down and cupped his cock. "And grown he has."

"I can't help that around you." He blushed.

He didn't get to finish that sentence before my lips were on his again.

CONNOR

It took over an hour before I got into town and found Kenny's pathetic excuse for a truck. What the hell did he buy with the money I gave him? Certainly not this piece of shit. Duct tape held pieces of the seat together, the windows didn't roll down, and something red and sticky was melting on the dashboard.

"Fucking pig."

Pushing the *Playboys* off the seat, I put the key into the ignition and the truck roared to life. By the sounds of it, the muffler was due to fall off at any moment.

"If I get pulled over for this piece of shit truck, Kenny, so help me fucking God."

Pulling out of the lot, I made my way into town. The "town" was laughable. There wasn't anything even close to a big box. None of the store names were recognizable. All mom-and-pop sounding places. Frustrated, I pulled into a parking spot, got out, and approached an old man sitting outside of what looked like a barbershop.

"Excuse me, sir. Would you happen to know where I could find a cell phone charger around here?"

"Cell phone, you say?" the man asked. He wore a white coat like a doctor might, with a pair of scissors poking out of the top of his front pocket. Just above that was the embroidered name of "Roger" in bright red thread.

"Yeah, or even any phone stores."

"Well, we ain't got one of them. Most folk around here still use a landline. You know what those are, son?"

I grit my teeth together. "Yeah, I know what a landline is. And I'm not your son."

Instead of being offended, the man just gave me a soft chuckle. "No, don't suppose you are. I'm a bachelor you see. No kids of my own. You got kids?"

"Look, Roger, I don't mean to be rude, but I'm in a terrible hurry. Do you know where I can get a phone charger or not?"

"The only place 'round here that might have what you need is a place called 'Upta Camp.' It's about a mile south of here. It's got a country store, but that's mostly food and gear. Essentials for the influx of camping folk we get, but they also have a gift shop, which might have what ya need."

"Perfect. Thank you. Which way is south from here?" I hated not having my phone's GPS to know how to navigate in this shit-nothing town.

"Right up that road a piece." He hitched his thumb to the road behind me. "They also got public showers and a laundromat," Roger said. He made a deliberate glance at my attire. "You know, for the hikers who get dirty on the trails."

"Thanks," I muttered. I probably was looking quite rough around the edges. Maybe a shower and getting all the blood and dirt out of my clothes wasn't a bad idea. It would take time to get plans in motion. Kenny was keeping watch, and it wasn't like they were about to leave now that they felt safe. Might as well take a second to clean up. I'd make sure to give my dick an extra scrub so that when I did kill Malcolm, I'd get a blow job from a very grateful Amanda.

CHAPTER FOURTEEN
Malcolm

My mouth was in disbelief as Amanda Fucking Jackson kissed me. Not just kissed me but indicated that she might have legitimate feelings for me. Still, I wasn't sure she was ready for what she was asking of me. The type of events she had been through would take her years and several therapists to heal even a fraction of the damage that monster and others in her life had done to her. I couldn't possibly take advantage of her fragile state of mind for my own selfish benefit. And yet, she and her hands had a magical way of persuasion.

"Amanda, what are you doing?"

She smiled at me coyly. "I'm just trying to make you more comfortable."

"By taking off my belt?"

"Well, you have to admit, belts are very uncomfortable, period. They dig into your stomach..."

"No. We can't. It's too soon. You need time to process."

Amanda pushed herself off me and quickly put her clothes back on. "If you didn't wanna fuck me you could have just said so."

"Amanda." I clenched my back molars to keep my volume calm. "Resisting you right now is one of the hardest things I've ever done. I have spent a good part of my youth fantasizing about what

I would do to you if I ever got the chance. But I also don't want to take advantage of the situation. I'm not saying I don't want to fuck you, because I absolutely do. I think you can see how much I want to." I pointed to my very erect penis. "But what I don't want is for you to regret this moment tomorrow. All I'm asking is to give yourself a little bit of time to make sure. I want you, Amanda. I'll make no bones about it, but I want all of you. Not just your body but your mind and your soul. I'm just asking for you to give it a little time for you to come to terms with all of the shit that's happened to you before we're intimate in that way."

From across the room, Amanda twiddled with the edge of her shirt. "How much time are we talking about?"

I couldn't help the laugh that escaped my lips. "However long it takes. If you need years, I'll give you that. I'll wait as long as you need. But when I finally get you in the bedroom, I want you to have no hesitation that it's me you want to be with. Deal?"

Amanda let free a dramatic sigh. "Fine. We won't fuck. I'll just be wet and horny for nothing."

I stood up and walked over to her, pressing my body dangerously close to hers. "I said that I wouldn't make love to you, not that I wouldn't eat you out."

Her eyes twinkled. "Really?" There was no mistaking the eagerness in her voice.

"Really." With consent given, I hoisted Amanda over my shoulder and carried her into the bedroom as she squealed in delight.

When we got into the darkened bedroom, I asked her if she wanted the light on or off.

"On. Definitely on. I want to see everything you're going to be doing to me."

"On it is. Bedroom lights on," I ordered. Automatically, the lights came on.

"Damn, your commanding voice is hot as hell."

Sitting her down on the bed, I smiled. "Oh yeah? Take your fucking shirt off before I rip it off you."

Amanda visibly shivered, and I wondered if I had taken it too far. She surprised me by biting on her lower lip gently.

"I'd like to see you try."

The challenge in her voice was unmistakable. But before I took her up on the challenge, she lifted her hands to cup both of her breasts through the fabric. She was deliberately toying with me. My hands moved on their own accord to shove hers aside.

"Mine." The words came out without my permission, but it was nonetheless true. "Take off your panties and lay down on the bed."

She smiled wickedly as she turned around so that her back was to me. Painfully slowly, she bent over as she slid the fabric over her ass, leaving me breathless.

My cock twitched, and it was all I could do not to rip my pants off and bury myself deep inside her. Shaking the image from my head, I gave her ass a quick spank. She squealed with delight before she climbed onto the bed and rolled onto her back.

Naked, save for the T-shirt she still had on, she lay there, extremely vulnerable. She looked up at me full of desire, and for a split second, I knew that she cared about me. Not just that she desired me but that she felt safe with me. It made my heart swell.

Without any prompting from me, she moved her hands down her thighs, landing on her knees, and then slowly spread herself wide, readying herself for my approach.

"Wishes do come true." I sighed, looking at her.

Just as I was lowering myself onto the bed, I heard an alarm sound. One of the parameters had been disturbed. Amanda shot up and grabbed a pillow to cover herself.

"What's that?" she whispered.

I reached down, grabbed her hand, and yanked her from the bedroom. I took her through the living room into the kitchen, opened the pantry, and slid open the false door to bring her inside the panic room once again. Once we had been safely locked inside, I let go of her hand and went over to the monitors.

"What's going on?" Fear laced her voice.

"It's probably just a deer. Or other wildlife. They trip the sensors quite often. They're highly sensitive. A strong wind could set it off."

She joined me in her scan of the monitors. Both of us searched for the thing we hoped we wouldn't find: Connor.

"How will you know what tripped it?" Her voice was still barely above a whisper.

She was scared, and I hated that I thought I was helpless to calm her at that moment because I didn't know for sure either. "There is a video feed that records on a twenty-four-hour loop. I'll need to watch over that tape to try to see what made the sensor go off, but it might take a little time. I should have looked over the footage earlier, honestly, but I didn't want to let you go." I glanced over at her, remembering how scared she had been. She had the same look now. "Right now, I'm just doing a quick scan of the access points."

"We're safe inside here though, right?"

"Yes. Even if he somehow managed to break inside the house, which is impossible to do from the outside, he's not getting into this panic room. Even if he knew it was here. Which he won't. We're behind a false wall. We're safe. Okay?"

She nodded, but it was clear she was still nervous as fuck. Until I watched the footage to confirm that it was just wildlife, I was just as on edge as her.

"Okay, I'm going to play back footage from the day we arrived on this monitor. You watch that. On this monitor, I'm going to watch this morning's feed. It'll be sped up, but if you see something, let me know and we can go back."

Amanda nodded. I hit a few keystrokes and got her footage going. She started watching with eagle eyes while I queued up the footage from this morning. The footage was recorded in thirty-second cycles, running from the front of the house to each side, before returning to the front again. I watched for several minutes as the sun slowly came up on the house. Nothing seemed out of the ordinary. The invisible fences were still up and working, although the battery life on my system seemed to have gone down a bar. Odd. It should be at full power. Clicking a few more keys, I checked on the transformer in the back. That's when I saw the tree. Right on top of the transformer. A smoking transformer. I looked back at the battery, which had dropped another bar. We were running on the generator backup.

"Fuck," I whispered. I expected Amanda to ask me what was going on, but when she didn't, I turned to check on her. Her face was white as a ghost as she watched something on the screen.

"What? What do you see?" I stood to get a better view of her screen. She just lifted her hand and pointed.

It was a shot of the driveway. At the top of the screen, Hodge's SUV was parked. Just the bottoms of his tires were visible in the shot.

"That's Hodge. He's one of my men. It's okay. He came to make sure the house was secure."

She shook her head and kept pointing. That's when I saw the shadow at the right of the vehicle. There were two sets of feet. The video had no audio and no way to pull back the footage to see who that other set of feet were, but when one set of bloody feet was lifted off the ground, the hairs on the back of my neck stood up. A moment later, the truck pulled out of the driveway. For one brief frame, we could see the driver of the SUV. Even from far away, and slightly blurry, there was no mistaking that face. It was Connor.

"He's here. He took out Hodge." I tapped a few more keys and frowned. "And killed our power. We're operating on the generator. But it's okay. We're safe. The doors are bank vault-style and locked from the inside. The locks to this room aren't generated by power. Neither are the front doors. There are no windows. He's not getting in here."

Amanda looked at me. The fear had left her face, replaced by something else. An emotion I couldn't quite read. Then, before I could even react, she opened the panic room door.

"Amanda, what are you doing?"

"I'm going to get food and go pee. We need to wait them out in here, right?"

"Yes, but I'll do that."

"You're going to go pee for me? Stay. Watch the monitors. Get the guns loaded. Yell if something happens. I'll be two feet away." I started to protest, but she put her finger up to stop me. "Either we're safe in here or we're not. Which is it?"

She was trying to call my bluff. If I wanted to keep her calm, I needed her to feel safer than we probably were. If Connor breached the house, the panic room would keep us safe, but only for so long. We'd eventually run out of food and water. He could easily wait us out. But she didn't need to know any of that.

"Okay. Fine. But hurry." My eyes went to the monitors inside the house as they tracked her going from the pantry to the bathroom. While she was in there, I scanned the footage again. If it was just Connor here, we might be okay. I had enough weapons in here to take down one guy.

My eyes went back to the inside monitors as Amanda emerged from the bathroom. From there she went into the living room where the go-bags were. She picked them up and then went to the kitchen. Placing one of the bags down she started to fill one of them with as much food as she could. She bent down to the lower cabinets, disappearing from view for a moment before she came back up with a twenty-four pack of water. She brought the water first and then went back to get the bag. The last thing she brought in was a bucket and toilet paper.

"Just in case," she said. She put the portable bathroom in the corner. She was smart. I wouldn't have thought about that necessity until it was too late.

Once she was inside, I shut the door behind her. With the additional items, it made the space even smaller.

Sitting down on the floor, she reached for the water and pulled out two bottles. She opened one and took a long pull, then she tossed one at me.

"Drink. I don't want you dehydrating in here. It's warm and

we're both sweating more than we probably feel comfortable admitting. If we're going to survive in here for the long term, we need to play this safe."

To appease her, I opened the bottle and downed nearly half the bottle. That seemed to satisfy her, so I went back to the monitors.

"Happy?" My eyes darted to each monitor, trying to determine where he'd taken Hodge.

"Come lay with me," she said. She reclined on the thin mattress.

"Amanda, I need to go over this footage before we lose the battery."

"Just for a minute. I need to feel your arms around me. I'm scared."

As much as I hated to admit it, I was too. Sure, I had weapons and a fortress to keep Connor out, but I also knew how cunning the man was. We might not be prepared for what he was planning.

She pulled her arms around her body, shivering, and I knew she was right. She needed assurance. Leaving my post, I stood up and stepped awkwardly over the bags that were stacked on top of each other. It took some effort, but I managed to lie down beside her on the floor. She tucked herself under my arm and rested her cheek on my chest.

"Thank you," she whispered. "Thank you for taking me away from Connor. For doing your best to try to keep me safe."

"You *are* safe." I sucked in a deep breath. The air in this room was not as fresh as it probably should be. It made the air feel thick. Heavy.

She propped herself up so that she was leaning on one elbow. With her other hand, she cupped my face. "I'm not safe. And we both know it. Connor's here. Probably his goons too. You and I both know he won't stop until he gets what he wants. His property." She pressed her lips to my forehead so tenderly, I closed my eyes against the sensation. "So, it's my turn to save you," she whispered.

My eyebrows pinched together. "What are you talking about?" I let loose a yawn that came out of nowhere.

"I think you know what I mean," she said. She stood. I tried to rise with her, but the room started to spin. The edges of my vision blurred.

"Amanda...what's going on?"

Amanda moved over to the monitors and held up the water bottle I'd practically downed. She gave me a small smile.

"I'm doing what you told me to do if Connor found us. I'm going to give myself up and protect you in the process." She walked over to the door as I fought to stand. It was a losing battle. She'd roofied me. Probably a double dose if I had to guess, based on how quickly my head was spinning.

"Amanda," I tried, but I struggled to keep my eyes open.

"Stay in this room, Malcolm. No matter what. Make sure we are long gone before you come out. You tried. And that's more than anyone else has ever done for me. But I won't sacrifice your life for mine."

"Amanda, please. Don't. I can get us—" I didn't get a chance to finish my sentence before my lids closed and the world went dark.

CHAPTER FIFTEEN

AMANDA

It might seem like what I was doing was stupid. Irrational. Insane. In reality, it was the only logical play. We were trapped. If I surrendered and threw myself at Connor's feet, acting so relieved that he'd saved me from Malcolm—as long as Malcolm stayed hidden—I might be able to save his life. That was the only thing that mattered to me.

Hence the roofie. Malcolm wouldn't have let me go through with this plan willingly. He would have fought me tooth and nail to stay inside that panic room. No. This time, I was going to save him.

I wasn't sure how long I had before the drugs wore off and Malcolm woke up and came out guns blazing, so I had to move fast. If Malcolm was right about the exits of the cabin, then I could at least get out, even if they couldn't get in. Both exits had massive vault-like wheels needed to open them. For my fake backstory to work that I was making up as I went, both doors would need to be open. I was going to tell Connor that I escaped while Malcolm was out. That way, they would know he wasn't still inside. It was the best I could do.

I opted to leave from the front door as I knew they were at

least watching that exit. I had no idea if I'd be shot on sight or if they'd swoop in and grab me. Either way, Malcolm stood a chance. Even if I died, they didn't know he was in that room, which meant he might live. And that was worth any price.

Swallowing my fears, I used all my strength, opened the front door, and ran. Hard. Like I was running away from a terrible monster. The performance of my life had begun, and I needed to sell every second of it.

With each step I took away from the safehouse the more the fear mounted. Tears welled in my eyes. These might be the last steps I ever took.

I kept waiting for Connor to appear from the bushes or for a bullet to take me down, but nothing came. So I kept running. Maybe he wasn't here, but he had been. I'd seen it from the cameras. Someone was watching me. Tracking my actions. Reporting back. I could feel it. I couldn't be seen going back to the safehouse now. I had to put distance between me and Malcolm.

At the end of the driveway, I had a choice. Left or right. I had no idea which direction we'd come from as I'd been out cold. To the right was all uphill, to the left was down. I opted for the easier path to run.

While the road was quiet, I wondered if I should attempt to stop any car that might pass by. The logic of my actions now would put Malcolm in danger if I played my hand wrong.

Would stopping cars for help make sense in the fictional story I was weaving? Ignoring a possible path to safety in this narrative seemed foolish. Especially if Connor's goons were tracking my movements. I could picture the conversation in my mind. *Yeah, boss, she passed like four cars but never once stopped to ask for help. Seems odd, right?*

"Stop right there." A voice came from the woods to my left. "Don't make another move." I froze. The voice wasn't Connor's or Malcolm's. A goon. I raised my hands in the air.

"Walk into the woods. Nice and slow."

Terrified, I did as I was told and got off the road to walk into the woods. Once the sun was no longer blinding me and my eyes adjusted to the darkness of the woods, I saw the man attached to the voice. He had what looked like some kind of sniper rifle pointed at my head. I didn't know much about guns other than I had no doubt he wouldn't miss if he pulled the trigger. He had on camo clothing and a baseball hat with long black greasy hair and a shaggy beard.

"On your knees," he said.

Shaking, I obeyed, wondering if this was it. If this was about to be my last moment on this planet. I tried my best to breathe slowly, in and out so I wouldn't faint. A second later something white and thin was tossed at me, landing a few inches from my knees. A zip tie.

"Put it on your ankles."

I let go a small sigh of relief. He wasn't going to kill me. At least not yet. He was making sure I didn't run. That was something. I shifted my weight to get to my ankles in front of me and placed the ties on them. My feet were bare, so there was no room to fake the ties being less than snug. Once those were secure, he bound my wrists with another tie.

Immobilized, he lowered the gun and let it hang across his chest by a shoulder strap. He reached to his neck and took off a red bandana he'd been wearing. He rolled it lengthwise and brought it to my lips.

"Open," he ordered.

Having no choice, I opened my mouth and let him shove the cloth inside as he tied the ends behind my head. I could taste the sweat on the bandana and pinched my eyes closed to fight back the tears. The man then tightened the zip ties, eliminating all hope of wiggling out of them later.

"Stay," he said. A small laugh escaped his lips.

The man reached into his back pocket and pulled out a cell.

"Fucking reception," he cursed. "We need to get to higher ground."

He walked over to me, shifted his gun, then lifted me off the ground and tossed me over his shoulder like a sack of potatoes. While I didn't know who this guy was, I knew he had to be linked to Connor. And if he was trying to make a call, that must mean Connor was very much keeping tabs on me. That was good. It meant that he at least cared if I lived or died. And if I had to be carried by a stranger to the top of this wooded area, fine by me. It would be even farther away from Malcolm, which I'd call a win.

For the better part of twenty minutes, I was jostled back and forth up the hill before the man set me down against a tree. He huffed a few times and wiped his forehead with the back of his arm before he pulled out his cell again.

"Finally. A signal."

Annoyed, he punched a button and then started tapping a message. A moment later, a buzz from his phone sounded. The man read the reply and nodded to himself.

"Looks like we need to wait for him to get a secure line." He walked closer to me and kicked my bound feet. "What do you think we should do to kill the time?"

The way his eyes shifted down my body I knew exactly how he'd want to pass the time. And I was helpless against whatever he had in mind.

"I can see why Connor is fighting so hard to get you back," he said appraisingly. "You ain't like his normal catch. You're a real woman. Not some rail-thin, barely legal chick. That ain't my style. I like a woman with some curves to her. And you got that, in spades." He ran the top of his gun down the curve of my jaw as I stood ramrod straight.

"Mmm, yeah," he said. He gazed at me as I stood helpless in just my T-shirt. "You have something to grab onto."

I pinched my eyes closed. I didn't want to see the lust growing in his eyes.

"Don't worry, Amanda. I'm not dumb enough to fuck you. Not if Connor has claimed you as his. But that's not to say I can't still get my rocks off before he gets here."

I felt him get closer to me. "Open your fucking eyes, woman. I want you to watch."

Knowing he had likely several weapons that could end my life, I did as he instructed. "That's right. Now, let's just lift this shirt off you, shall we?"

My teeth ground together as I tried to shove him away with my bound hands.

"Stop fighting me, or I'll put a bullet right between those perfect breasts."

I had no choice. I had to let him finish with me. The sooner he was done, the better. He reached down at the fabric of the white T-shirt and lifted it over my head.

"Damn, woman. No panties either? No wonder that boy is pistol-whipped." He undid his belt and his pants dropped to the ground. Reaching into his boxers, he pulled free his cock. I focused my eyes on the ground beside him as he ran his left hand over my body, latching his gross fingers on my breast as he jacked himself off with his right. The only saving grace was that he was a two-pump chump. It was over almost as fast as it had started.

After he'd panted his way back into normal breathing and put himself away, he grabbed my breast again, hard.

"Not a fucking word about this to Connor, or I'll find you and skin you alive. And I'll cut this tit off as a trophy. Understood?"

I nodded quickly. I didn't doubt his threat for a moment.

He lowered the shirt back over my head just as his cell started to ring.

"Ya. I got her. She ran out of the house and down the road. She looked shaken. Yeah, yeah. I got her in a secure spot. Not sure if Malcolm is in the house or not. Opted to follow the prize instead."

My heart started to race at the thought of this man going to try and hunt Malcolm down.

The man looked over at me and frowned. "Ya, I'll put her on. Just a second." He walked over to me and mouthed 'Not a word.' I nodded before he removed the bandana and lifted the phone to my lips.

Time to sell the biggest lie I'd ever tell.

CONNOR

Still dripping wet from the shower, I yanked the charging cord that I'd purchased at the gift shop out of the outlet. I was already packing to leave. Had Kenny really found her?

"Connor?" Amanda's voice was shaky, but there did seem to be...relief.

"Amanda? Are you okay? Are you hurt?" I couldn't believe I was asking that. Allowing myself to care about her well-being, but I had to know what I was dealing with.

"I'm okay. Just scared. I knew you'd find me. I kept telling Malcolm that you would, but he wouldn't listen. Where are you? Can you come rescue me?"

Rescue. That meant she hadn't gone with him willingly. "Amanda, I need you to listen to me very carefully. Did Malcolm hurt you?"

"No. I'm okay. He thought he was saving me from you, but I told him over and over that I didn't want to leave. I didn't want to leave you. I was trying to get back to you. I swear." I could hear the tears in her eyes. My heart swelled, getting confirmation that she hadn't run from me.

"Where is he now?"

"I don't know. I woke up and he was gone. I saw the side door open. I don't know, maybe he went to get food or firewood? I just knew I wouldn't have long before he came back, so I just bolted. I was going to try and find a phone or something. Try to find my way back to you. But I don't know where the hell I am. We've been driving for so long."

My teeth ground together. "I know where you are, baby. I'm on my way. Until then, Kenny will keep you safe. Put him back on the line now for me."

A moment later the phone shuffled and Kenny came back on.

"Any sign of Malcolm leaving?"

"No boss. I didn't see anything, but who knows? Maybe he has some elaborate underground tunnel system or some shit?"

"Where are you now?"

"I'm at the top of the hill. The only place that has reception."

"Keep her there," I said. "I'm on my way."

"Ten-four."

Ending the call, I let loose a sigh. She was safe. And she had been trying to get back to me. I hated how much relief that brought me.

I was in Kenny's truck and on the road back in less than twenty minutes. My hair was still dripping wet, and my clothes were sticking to my body from not drying off well enough, but I didn't care. All that mattered was Amanda was safe. I needed to see her. I needed to look into her eyes and see for myself that she was happy to see me. Feel her in my arms. Only then would I trust that this wasn't some elaborate act.

Pulling into Malcolm's driveway like a bat out of hell, I made no attempt to cover my arrival. If Malcolm was inside, I wanted him to know I was there. His days were numbered to the second.

I pulled out my cell and walked right up to one of his cameras. "I'm here. Bring her to the house. The door's still open. We're gonna go on a manhunt."

"Give me five," Kenny said.

I put my phone in my pocket and took out my gun. Instinct told me I should wait for Kenny before I went in to scope out the place, but I had to see for myself if the bastard was inside or not.

Slowly, I entered the house. The massive door that was easily a foot thick was ajar enough to let me in without touching it. There was a small living space with a couch, a fireplace, and a chair. Beyond that, there was another room. The door was open, but the lights were off. Moving like a snail, I approached the room, ready to take fire at anything that moved. After a quick scan, I could tell it was a bedroom from the light spilling in from the living room. Finding the light switch, I turned it on to make out a single queen bed. A pair of handcuffs were on the nightstand. This is where he kept her locked up. My blood boiled.

There were no closets, and there was nothing under the bed. The kitchen was empty, as was the pantry, though it was well stocked with food. "Looks like you have plenty of food, Malcolm, so where did you run off to..."

Unless he was still inside.

Narrowing my attention, I went to the last room. The bathroom. That too was empty. That's when I noticed that the back exit was open, just as Amanda said. So maybe he did go for wood? The vehicle he brought Amanda in was still in the driveway, so if he left, it was on foot.

Whipping around, I lifted the gun and knelt by the couch. If Malcolm walked back into the house, it would be the last thing he ever did.

For the next several minutes, I held my ground. That's when I heard the sound of footsteps. Only one set. They sounded heavy too. I narrowed my eyes to get a clear shot and very nearly took out Kenny.

"Jesus Christ, Kenny. Why didn't you say something? I almost shot you." That's when I saw why there was only one set of footfalls. He had Amanda over his shoulder. Her feet and hands were zip-tied.

"Sorry man, I didn't know you were inside."

"Put her down," I barked. Kenny walked over to the couch and placed her on the cushions. Her eyes lit up when she saw me. I hated how my heart flipped at the reaction.

"Take that fucking gag off her."

Kenny took out a knife and cut it off her.

"You came," she cried as she stood up. "I can't believe you're really here." Her arms lifted as though she wanted to hug me, but because she was tied, she couldn't wrap them around me. I did a strange thing then, got on my knees and ducked my head so she could slip her arms around my neck. She squeezed me so hard that I thought I might cry. *She is happy I'm here.*

"Shhh, baby. You're safe now." Out of the corner of my eye, I noticed Kenny shift uncomfortably. He was seeing way too much of my vulnerable side. Shaking myself out of it, I moved her arms back. "Let me look at you. I want to make sure you're not hurt." I scanned her body to check for injuries. Nothing seemed out of place, except... "What's this green shit on your shirt?"

Amanda's eyes widened a fraction of a second. She looked at Kenny but then quickly looked to the ground.

"Kenny? What is this?"

Kenny shifted again. "Probably some of my camo paint. Not like I got a bathroom to wash my hands out here." He held them up to confirm, showing bits of green and brown paint covering his gross fingers.

"Yes, but why is *your* paint on her shirt?" I lifted my gun to his head.

"I don't know. Some probably came off as I was catching her from runnin' or maybe it's from the hog tyin' or liftin' her to get to you."

I cocked my head. The way he spoke I could tell he was nervous. "Did you touch her?"

It was clear what I meant by my question, as Kenny took a step back. "No man. I didn't. I swear."

Leaving my gun pointed at Kenny, I looked at Amanda.

"Did he lay a finger on you?"

Amanda's big blue eyes widened before she sighed and lifted her shirt. Her left breast was covered in green and brown camo paint, leaving behind clear fingerprints of Kenny's hand on my property.

I pulled the trigger and dropped Kenny in one shot. Amanda screamed. My teeth ground together in anger. "What did he do?" I seethed.

There was no point in beating around the bush. "He felt me up as he jacked off. Said if I told anyone he'd skin me alive and keep my breast as a trophy."

Two more shots into Kenny's limp body. While he may not have fucked her, he touched her. He touched what was mine and that meant death.

"Malcolm's next."

CHAPTER SIXTEEN

AMANDA

He killed his goon. Right in front of me. No hesitation. Just boom. Dead. That told me two things. One, he still felt possessive over me, which I could use to my advantage. But also, that he would have no trouble pulling the trigger on me if I said or did the wrong thing. If any one of my lies was unbelievable, I was a goner. If I wasn't terrified before, I was now.

Closing my eyes, I shimmed over to Connor with my still-bound hands and feet and leaned my head against him, and I started to cry. That part was easy. I was scared shitless.

"Thank God you found me," I whimpered into his chest. I pressed my body as hard as I could into his, mostly so that I wouldn't have to look him in the eyes. If he studied me too closely, he might see the fear lingering there.

At first, he was tense against my chest, but then he placed his free hand on my hips and squeezed his fingers into my flesh so hard, I knew they would leave a mark.

"I always come for what's mine, Amanda." He whispered his words into my hair, and I let loose a shaky breath. I knew at that moment that I was never going to be free. Unless I found a way to kill him.

Connor pulled me back then, forcing my eyes on him.

Thankfully, they still had tears he could mistake as relief and not fear. "I'm going to find him, Amanda. And when I do, I'm going to make him suffer for what he did to you."

Goosebumps ran down my neck. "Can we go now?"

"Not until I'm satisfied. Now sit your ass on the couch."

"Yes, Master," I said, quickly submitting. I'd pushed too hard and now I needed to be submissive as fuck.

"I'm going to check the rooms again. Make sure I didn't miss anything."

I nodded quickly as my heart beat fast in my chest. I held my breath when he searched the pantry and didn't take another until he reemerged into the living room. He went into the bedroom and came out with the handcuffs Malcolm had used.

"Are these what he used on you?" I nodded. He seemed to mull that answer over. "What did you attach you to?"

"Nothing. Just my hands together."

"So you could still run then. Why didn't you?"

Fuck. He was trying to find flaws in my story already.

"I tried. A few times," I said, which wasn't untrue. "But he overpowered me. Then he started drugging me when we traveled. At night he zip-tied our feet together." I came up with that lie thanks to my current situation.

"Smart. A tactic I might have to start employing. And you're sure he never touched you? I swear to God, Amanda, if he fucked you..."

"He didn't." Which was true. We'd had oral and done lots of kissing and foreplay, but as of yet, his cock had never entered me.

"Something in your story isn't lining up, Amanda." Connor's eyes narrowed onto me and my blood ran cold.

"What?" My voice came out dry.

"I can understand you running from Malcolm. From being locked up. But why would you want to run back to me? To your cage? No sane person wants to be in a cage, Amanda. So tell me the truth," he said. He pulled the gun out and held it under my jaw. The cold metal pressing against my skin chilled me to the core.

I looked him dead in his eyes and swallowed all my fear. "I didn't want to go back for the cage. I wanted to go back to you."

"Me?"

Nodding. "You know how much my body responds to yours. I can't help it. I'm drawn to you. Like a magnet."

With the gun still pressed against my jaw, I saw his eyes soften. A moment later, his hand was cupping my breast. I gasped, trying my best to make it sound sexy and not scared.

"You don't want me, Amanda." His voice was low. "I'm dangerous. Cruel. Possessive."

"I know. But don't you see why that's such a turn-on? You came here. You traveled across the country to find me. You killed a man because he dared to touch me. *Your* property. You want me in a way no other man has. You make me feel like I matter. It doesn't hurt that your cock is the best dick of my life." Again, not a lie, but not the full truth either. It was the only way through. Partial truths. Otherwise, he'd see right through me. I had to play to his ego. It seemed to be working. For now.

A small smile danced on his lips. He placed the gun in the waistline of his pants, then reached into his pocket for a jackknife. The switchblade popped open, and I flinched against the sound. Connor grabbed my wrists and quickly sliced through the tie.

"Once Malcolm is dead," Connor said. He rubbed the red marks on my wrists gently. "I'm going to bury him, then bury my cock so deep inside of you, you'll see stars."

I closed my eyes and moaned. "See, that's what I'm talking about. That's fucking hot."

"I've never owned a pet before, Amanda, but you make it so damn hard to resist." He ran his fingers along the side of my face. Keeping my eyes closed so he wouldn't see the disgust, I pressed my face to his touch, knowing that's what he'd expect me to do.

"And I've never had someone so protective of me." Opening my eyes, I tried to look into his and see the broken and beaten-down boy who had grown into the monster before me. I had to remember that I once felt drawn to him. Before I'd met Malcolm. Before I knew what real men were like.

Connor wasn't dumb. He'd know if I was playing him. This had to be convincing. Lifting my hand, I traced my fingertips down his chest. Breathing through the motion. "Maybe we can both enjoy this new experience together." He looked down at my hand and took it in his. Perhaps it was working.

"I need to work now." He reached down and picked up the cuffs from the bedroom. He cuffed the hand that was on his chest. "We can play later."

My eyes grew wide as I saw the cuff on my wrist again.

"What's wrong? Don't you trust me?" There was a slight edge to his voice.

"No. Of course, I do. It's just that I probably should have warned you that I don't know where the key is," I said quickly. He led me up from the couch and to the bedroom.

"Well, that is a shame. Hmm. You may have to live in cuffs," he said. He slipped the other one on my empty wrist. "Now that's an idea." He shook his head once and pointed to the bed. "You are a distraction. Get in bed. And don't lift an ass cheek off of it until I tell you to. Understood?"

"Yes, Master."

"Good girl."

Connor's use of the phrase did not send warm sensations through me as it had with Malcolm. Instead, all I felt were shivers.

Doing as I was told, I climbed on the bed as best I could with my hands cuffed in front of me, once again a prisoner. I had to remind myself that this time it was my choice. If this act meant I could save Malcolm, then I had to try. But we also needed to get the hell out of this house before Malcolm woke up, because there was no telling what Malcolm would try once he realized what was going on.

MALCOLM

Blinking awake on the floor of the panic room, I tried in vain to piece together the moments from when I'd downed the water Amanda had given me to the moment I woke up alone on the ground. It was hard because everything still felt like it was spinning.

That's when I heard a voice coming through one of the monitors. Deep and angry. Connor.

With my heart racing, I sat up and looked around the room. Amanda was gone, the panic room door sealed shut. Her plan came back to me in a wave. Sacrifice herself to save me.

I stood up as quietly as I could so as not to give away my advantage. Stealth-like, I went over to the monitor to assess the situation. Coming out guns blazing might lead to Amanda being in the crossfire, and I couldn't risk that.

A quick scan of the monitors that were now at thirty percent battery life showed me Amanda was in the bedroom. It was dark, so I couldn't make out if she was conscious or not, but my hunch was that Connor wouldn't come all this way just to kill her. He'd want to at least interrogate her first.

My eyes then diverted to the porch camera where Connor was standing. He had a cell phone in his hand and was shouting at someone. I didn't want to risk turning up the volume any further in case he heard an echo of his voice, so instead, I pressed my ear to the speaker.

"I don't care what you're in the middle of. I need you to get some men here to get rid of the body. Well, both bodies. I have another inside an SUV just down the road from here. That will need to be scrubbed too. Once those are taken care of, set a match to this place."

I watched Connor as he paced. It was evident his mind was working a mile a minute to clean up the very big mess that he had made in the short time he was here. But was there anyone else with him?

"How far away are you?" Connor asked, providing the answer to his unspoken question for him.

"Twelve hours? How the fuck are you twelve hours away?" Connor kicked at the post on the porch. "I can't fucking wait that long. I need to get Amanda back in her cage and check on the others. I shouldn't have been gone this long." He ran his free hand over his face, which was already starting to grow some stubble. "Okay, this is what's going to happen. I'm going to leave Kenny's body in the house. You need to get Hodge inside. Pull the teeth on both. Cut off the fingers. Take those to the firepit. I'll let them know to expect a delivery. Leave nothing traceable to them. Then light the fucking house up and leave." Another kick to the post. "Yeah, I'll be heading out now. Got Kenny's piece-of-shit truck. I'll offload that somewhere, then fly back. Questions?"

Connor looked around the woods and pinched a hand to his brow. "Fuck if I know. Malcolm seems to have ghosted. Maybe he saw Kenny and got spooked. Saved himself? I don't know. I don't have time to wait around and find out. He's either bailed or he's lying in wait. If it's the latter, I'm a sitting duck without backup."

So he was alone. Perfect. Connor nodded a few times as he continued to pace. "In the meantime, I need this mess sorted. If you pull this off, Diaz, you'll be promoted. No fuck-ups. Understood?"

Connor pushed the "end" button and shoved the phone back in his suit jacket. He knelt into a low squat and cradled his head in his hands for a moment before he let loose a long, slow breath.

"Get her home, lock her up, and never let her out of my sight again. Malcolm will not be the reason my empire falls," he said to himself.

He stood up then and walked back inside. He glared around the living room. I turned off the volume on the monitor, grabbed one of the guns in the back, slid in a clip, and winced against the click it made. I released the safety and pressed my back against the door on the off-chance Amanda didn't close the false wall in the pantry all the way.

I could hear his feet as they scuffled around the house. I didn't dare breathe for fear he'd hear me inside. I wasn't worried about what he'd do to me but what he would do to Amanda if he even suspected she'd been hiding me.

And that's when it hit me. That's exactly what she was doing. She was enacting the plan I told her to do if Connor caught her. That meant I had to live up to my end of that bargain to not blow my cover and stay alive so I could rescue her on my terms. I knew where he was holding her now, so I already had the upper hand. I just had to sit fucking tight and not move from this goddamn spot no matter what.

"Who the fuck eats puffed rice?" Connor asked mere inches from my head. Jesus. He was in the pantry.

"Fucking health nut," Connor spat. "No fucking protein in half this shit. Pathetic."

There were some sounds of food being tossed to the ground and spilling onto the floor. But eventually, his footfalls left the pantry.

Letting free a breath, I waited a moment to make sure the coast was clear before I quietly got up and went back to the bank of screens. One of them had already cut out. The generator was failing. It was designed to shut off smaller systems first, leaving the locks for last. Not that I needed them now that we'd already been breached.

That's when I saw the top of Connor's head at the camera covering the living room. A moment later, that feed died too. Shit. It wasn't the generator killing the camera. He was killing the feed one at a time. Fucker was covering his bases.

I waited in frustration as he cut every single feed, save one. The bedroom where Amanda was kept. My pulse quickened as he walked into her room and flicked on a light. She was sitting on the bed, her legs bound at the ankles. Handcuffs on her wrists on her lap, sitting tall.

"Someone's been a good girl," he said. He ran his fucking fingers along her jaw, pulling her face upward to look at him. The way the camera was angled, they were both in profile, so I could see the fear that she was working so hard to mask.

"To reward you for following orders, I'm going to fuck you so hard your teeth will rattle." Connor shocked me then by looking right at the camera. "And Malcolm, wherever he is, will have this footage waiting for him to find I've taken back my property." He turned back to the camera. "She's *mine*, Malcolm. You hear me? Mine."

My blood ran cold as I watched Amanda's reaction. The abject terror was there while Connor's gaze was on the camera but vanished into a practiced desire by the time he'd looked back at her.

She was about to endure hell to keep me safe. My head spun again as I tried to clear my head. I had to get a grip on what this asshole was going to make me sit here and watch. While I was awake, I was in no way prepared to face Connor. The drugs were very much still in my system because my balance was not great. I'd need to be at the top of my game if I wanted to take him down. And Amanda knew that. So she was going to let him have her to save me.

CHAPTER SEVENTEEN

AMANDA

There was nothing I could do but be an active and willing participant in whatever Connor wanted to do to me. The man had beef with Malcolm and wanted to make him suffer in every way possible. Little did he know that watching this act would probably hurt Malcolm more than any physical torture Connor wished upon him. The fact that I had to make my reciprocation convincing made it even worse.

Just as Connor's hands were about to tear against my shirt, his cell rang. Cursing, he picked it up and shoved me onto the bed.

"This better be important or someone is losing a head," Connor seethed. From my spot on the bed, I watched as his shoulders tensed. His eyes darted toward the front door and then he cursed again. A moment later, he was tucking his phone in his pocket.

"Fuck. Change of plans. Someone was hiking in the woods and heard the gunshots. Cops are on the way. We gotta leave. Now." He reached down and hoisted me over his shoulder, my hands still cuffed, my feet still bound. He carried me outside to an old beat-up pickup.

"Get on the floor. Keep your head down," he barked as he shoved me inside the truck.

Malcolm had me do the same thing, but this truck had far less legroom to curl myself up in. Being cuffed didn't make things any easier.

Connor didn't bother to wait until I was in a comfortable spot before he was reversing out of the driveway. He pulled off the road a few moments later. Then, he put the truck in park. "Stay here. I need to do one thing. If you try to run, so help me fucking God, Amanda..."

"I won't run. I'm right where I want to be," I said with as much conviction as I could muster.

A second later, the truck door slammed, and I heard the sound of his feet crunching against the gravel. Once the sounds retreated, I risked pushing myself up to look out the window. I saw him heading for the woods, where he must have parked the SUV. A moment later, there was a loud boom and a great ball of fire erupted. Shrieking, I shrank back onto the floor, and a few minutes later, Connor was back inside the truck. His eyes found me, and he nodded once as though relieved I was still here.

"What was that noise?"

"I had to get rid of some evidence. I didn't have time for my normal cleanup. Kenny's body will have to stay where it is. But it's good. Now his death can be tied to the owner of the house. One Malcolm Luxx." He grinned, then pulled out onto the road and drove in silence for several minutes.

If the cops were coming and Malcolm was still inside, they'd take him in for questioning...and if they did any digging into his very illegal past, they'd lock him up. There would be no rescue mission.

"We're gonna have to dump this truck," Connor said after we were on the road for several minutes. "I'll book us a flight, get us back to—" He turned then and stared down at me. "Did you tell him about where you were being held?"

I shook my head, hoping it wasn't too long of a delay. "No. Why would I?"

Connor shook his head. "Why wouldn't you, is the question. I can't figure you out, Amanda. Malcolm was offering you freedom. And you're seriously trying to sit here and tell me that you wanted to give that up? For me? What's your angle?"

"My angle? I don't have an angle. I told you. It was for you."

"Yeah, and that's a little too convenient for me. Is it for the other women? Is that it? Are you trying to get back there to save them? Because I'll tell you this right now, Amanda, there is no saving them. Their fates are sealed."

"What? No!" I protested, my voice breaking slightly.

"Then what is it? Why run from Malcolm if he wasn't hurting you?"

He was doubting my motives. Which he had every right to. This plan of mine made no sense at all. He'd see through the guise in no time. I had to think of something, and fast.

"Look, Connor, I know you won't believe this. But Malcolm, as kind as he was...as well-intentioned his motives might have been, they weren't what I wanted. I'm damaged. You know that. Our childhoods made sure that we'd never live normal lives. I know this is hard to believe, but I *wanted* you to take my power from me. I *wanted* to be submissive, but only with you. Malcolm wanted to treat me like his equal. Which is the type of guy I should probably want. But I found myself craving your hands on my body. Craved your cock driving inside of me. I wanted those dangerous eyes to rake over me like they wanted to devour me. I don't want a normal relationship. I want someone who will make my whole body come alive. And the only person who has ever done that to me, ever, has been you. Who wouldn't try to run to find it again?"

Connor tilted his head, contemplating my words, so I tried to cement my logic. "I get that it doesn't make any sense to want you, Connor. I know who you are. I know what you do for a living. I should be appalled by you. But I'm not. I hate myself for it, but I want to be with you. For as long as you'll allow it. Even if it's only for this drive back to my cage. I'll take it. I just want to be with you."

He was quiet for a moment while he pondered. "You're either the dumbest woman on the planet or the smartest. I can't decide which."

I forced a laugh. "The dumbest. For sure."

"Keep your head down. We're about to go through the town. Once we clear that, I'll let you come up and sit beside me."

"Yes, Master."

I saw him flinch. "Amanda... Call me Connor."

My heart leapt at the slight victory. "Okay, Connor." I pulled my lips into a smile, and I swear, I saw his lips do the same, if only for a second. This was the role I had to keep up. Or he would end me. And there was no telling what he'd do to Malcolm when he finally found him. I had to keep us both safe and be the best actress that ever was.

The jostling of the truck, combined with the hum of the engine and general exhaustion from the last few days, must have caused me to drift off, because when I awoke, it was dark out. I had no idea what time it was or even where we were.

The truck door opened on my side and Connor's arms quickly had me cradled against his chest. The handcuffs clinked against themselves, reminding me how very much a prisoner I was.

"Where are we?" I was trying to get my bearings. Data that might be useful somehow.

"It doesn't matter. We're hopping on a plane. You'll be home soon."

"Home," I murmured before nestling my face against his chest. I felt him stiffen slightly against me. I wondered if I'd overdone it, but then he relaxed into it.

"You can sleep more on the flight."

He carried me up the steps of a small plane that we'd parked beside. I had no idea even what state we were in but if he was taking me back to Luxx, at least Malcolm would know where to find me. Presuming the cops didn't detain him when they arrived at the safehouse.

On the plane, he sat me down on one of the chairs, and he collapsed into the one across from me. He looked exhausted. After a moment he said, "Let me help you with your seatbelt." I did my best not to flinch when his fingers touched my stomach to bring the clasp together.

"I've never been on a plane before," I said. Staring out the window, I tried to pick up some context clues about where we were.

"Nothing to it. The flight will only be a few hours." He leaned back and buckled his own.

"You look like you haven't slept in days." I watched his face as he closed his eyes.

"I haven't." He cracked his eyes open. "I've been hunting for you."

I smiled because I knew that was expected. "And I'm so grateful you did. I wasn't sure if Malcolm had bought and paid for me or if..."

"No. He stole you. And no one steals from me and lives for long." The ice in his voice was palpable.

"So what happens now?"

"Now, we sleep." He closed his eyes, shutting down all discussion. Handcuffed on a private plane, there wasn't much I could do either. It wasn't like I could escape. The pilot was on Connor's payroll, so even if I tried to beg for help it would be denied. There was a gun in Connor's holster, but I'd never shot a gun before. Bound and on an airplane was probably not the day to learn. So I did the only other thing I could think to do. I slept.

CONNOR

We would land in a few minutes, so I knew I needed to wake her up, but I couldn't stop looking at her. Her knees were pulled into her chest and her arms hugged them close to her. I knew the unconscious sleep position well. It was a result of trauma. Make yourself as small and unnoticeable as possible. For me, it was also the only way to sleep when Mother locked me in the cage. I could still hear her words of wisdom whenever she shut me in for disobedience.

"I'm doing this for your own good, Connor. You must learn how to control the people in your life. Like you would a pet. The people in your life are yours to command, but only if you show that you are the suppressor. Once you learn this, you will never be caged again."

She was right of course. It was her teachings that gave me the idea of the foster setup. From my mother, I learned dominance. With a bit more training, Amanda would make the ideal pet. Which is what Amanda was asking me for. She wanted to submit to me. Would I allow her to become mine in every sense of the word?

As tempting as the idea was, there was also the other half of my genetics to consider. Where my mother had been the one with meticulous control, my father had shown me the ultimate form of weakness. Someone who gave his power over to temptation. First to my mother, then to the bottle, and now, to the gambling. He lacked any self-discipline. He had been powerless against my mother, and if I were to let Amanda in...if I were to take her on as my pet, I could see myself giving my power over to her. And I would not be put back into a cage. No. I couldn't do that. My power was mine. I would never relinquish it. Never again.

Ultimately, I had to get rid of Amanda. It was the only logical choice. But I also had to hold onto her. I refused to let her go. Which meant there was no clear path to take. She already held too much control over me. The only thing I knew for certain was that

I needed to get her back in her cage. Then I could think about what to do next. One shitshow at a time.

The landing gear came down then, jostling Amanda awake. At first, her eyes were fearful as she took in her surroundings, but when her doe eyes found mine, she smiled. She fucking smiled. And damn it all if it didn't make my heart speed up. She was going to be a problem.

"We're here. A car should be waiting for us. It's almost over."

Amanda nodded and looked out the window. Her eyes were bright and, dare I say it, happy. To be here. With me. It made no sense.

"Once we get back to the compound, I'll need to put you back in your cage."

The brightness left her eyes. That was more like it. That's how she should look at me.

"Oh," she said quietly.

"My father is at my place." I didn't know why I'd felt the need to explain myself to her. "I wasn't sure if he'd be safe with Malcolm being rogue. And because the fucker is still alive somewhere, I need to keep my dad protected. I don't know what sort of thugs he has, but I wouldn't put it past him to try and take my father as some pathetic attempt to trade his life for yours. As though I care that much for my father," I scoffed. "But that's hardly the point. That man is done taking things that belong to me. So, for now, he'll be staying at my place where I can keep an eye on him. Once that's sorted, we can try keeping you at my place."

That news seemed to please her. She wore a small smile again. It killed me how much I liked seeing it there.

When we were in the car, I used a pair of bolt cutters I'd asked to have at the ready to remove the handcuffs from Amanda's wrists. I cut the ties at her feet as well.

Our driver said it would take about twenty minutes to get to our destination. I could have waited until we got her back in her cage, but I didn't want to risk anyone seeing the cuffs once we got out of the car. I didn't need any attention on me or my building at the moment.

"Thank you," she said. The SUV moved us forward. She rubbed her hands across the red marks the cuffs had left behind. "Now I can finally do this," she whispered, pushing free of her seat and dropping to her knees in front of me.

My eyes darted to the driver, who had been well-trained to keep his eyes on the road. As much as I should have restricted this play time to when we were safely in her cage, my cock disagreed. Just the idea of her lush lips being around it had me growing hard.

"Miss me?" I heard myself laugh.

"So much," she admitted, reaching her hands up my thighs and up to my belt, undoing it with practiced ease. Eagerly, I lifted my ass off the seat while she pulled my pants down past my knees.

My cock jumped to attention, ready for her expert lips to be on me. It was so dangerous, giving her this much power. I knew it, and yet, I wasn't about to stop her. I wanted this. No, *needed* this to happen.

The second her lips were on my dick, my eyes rolled back in my head. She was unbelievably skilled. When her hands joined in and started to caress my balls, it was too much. She knew how to get me off in ways no other woman had even come close to. Reaching into my jacket pocket I grabbed my cell and snapped a picture of her between my thighs. A fun image to share with Malcolm one day.

Amanda's skill at knowing just how tightly to press her lips around my shaft and how hard to squeeze my balls was unparalleled. She was sucking on me no longer than a few minutes before I was blowing my load against her skilled tongue.

"Fuck!" My hips bucked off the seat so she could take every last inch of me inside of her. She swallowed all of me down, sucking ever so gently as I came down from the high, licking me dry. My body shuddered as she withdrew her warmth.

Panting, I watched as my dick seemed to wave in surrender.

She had my number. I was too weak around her. I needed to get a grip on myself. And on her.

"Put my dick back in my pants and then get your ass back in the seat, and don't move again unless I tell you to," I ordered.

Her eyes shifted from delight to worry as I barked the order at her. As it should be. I can't let her get too comfortable around me. *If* she stood any chance of becoming my pet, she would have to be ready to do my bidding. I owned her. Not the other way around.

I would put her to the test. If she could follow orders...then maybe, maybe, I could keep her. Maybe.

After I found Malcolm and killed the bastard, of course.

CHAPTER EIGHTEEN

MALCOLM

If what I'd overheard Connor say about the cops being on the way was true, I knew my time hiding inside was limited. The last thing I needed was for the cops to know anything at all about me. And if they came into the house, they would soon know far more about me than I wanted. My prints would be all over everything. And with a dead body in the house, I didn't exactly want to have any connection to that. Which left one option. An idea I took from Connor himself: torching the place.

I rifled through the go-bags, taking only what I could realistically get on a flight. None of the weapons, only one passport, some cash, a couple of burners... The rest would have to be sacrificed to the fire.

Still groggy from the roofie, I tossed the much lighter bag over my shoulder and took one last look around the cabin. Then, I gave the dead guy a kick to make sure he was dead. Being burned alive was a fate I wished on no one. Not even one of Connor's hired guns.

Satisfied, I turned on the gas to the stove—more specifically, the burner with the broken starter. The scent of propane wafted to my nose, alerting me to the invisible danger filling the kitchen.

Once I was outside, I waited and watched the propane tank

empty inside the house. It was taking far longer than I would have thought. I waited as long as I could until I heard sirens in the distance. It was now or never. Digging around in the go-bag for a book of matches. I lit the whole book and set ablaze a large branch I'd found on the ground. The blast from this explosion would be loud and dangerous. I had to be as far away from it as humanly possible. But that propane would need a spark to ignite.

Running as deep into the woods as I thought my aim would allow, I hauled back and threw my make-shift torch at the back door that I'd left slightly ajar. The torch fell to the ground about a foot away from the entrance and nearly extinguished itself. But, after a moment, the wood steps beneath it caught fire. Perfect. It would find its way inside, and when it did, I'd be far enough away to not be harmed.

Not wanting to push my luck, I bolted up the hill. No less than three minutes later, a huge explosion rocketed into the air. Turning, I saw the smoke. Mission accomplished.

That should pull the focus of authorities to the fire long enough for me to make my way out of the woods. There was an escape route for a situation just like this. My backup plans had backups. I trusted nothing.

Pausing at the top of the hill, the sirens grew louder, so I took the opportunity to try calling Darcy. She picked up on the third ring.

"Status?" she asked.

"I need a flight home, STAT. And a car to whatever airport you find."

"What happened to the truck we got you?"

"It's currently on fire. As is the safehouse."

I could hear the sound of a keyboard clicking. "Of course it is," she said. "Okay, I have two tickets that leave in four hours—"

"I just need one."

"Oh..."

I pressed my fingers against the bridge of my nose and closed my eyes for a moment. "He took her, Darcy. He fucking took her. He found us and he took her."

Darcy didn't speak for a moment. "Are you hurt?"

Naturally, she assumed I must be hurt if I let Connor take Amanda away. I would have made that leap too.

"No. Amanda slipped me a roofie when she found out Connor was at the cabin. She hid me in the panic room and let him take her to save me."

"Wow. That's..."

"Stupid. Very," I said. Rolling my shoulders, I tried to rid my body of the tension.

"I was going to say that's love."

"That's taking it a bit far."

"Is it?" Darcy asked. "She willingly went back into the arms of her captor just to make sure you came out of this situation unharmed. I don't even know if Camila would do something like that for me. That's some next-level connection. Just how tight did the two of you get on this road trip?"

"Tight enough that I can't let her be caged again. I'm busting her out."

"And just how are you going to do that?"

I sighed. "I don't know yet. I'll figure it out on the plane. Text me the deets on the travel home."

"Already sent," she said.

Looking down at my phone, I saw that there was a booking for a flight leaving in about two hours and an address of where to meet the one and only cab driver in a fifty-mile radius.

"You need a raise," I said.

"Yes, I do."

Laughing, I let her know I'd be in touch and then dropped the phone on the ground, broke the screen, and removed the SIM card. I tossed the bits inside the go-bag next to a new burner phone and headed toward the coordinates for my cab.

There wasn't a lot of time to come up with a plan to rescue Amanda once again from Connor. Running from him wasn't the answer because his network of thugs was smarter than I expected them to be. My first thought was the obvious one: to call in an anonymous tip. Clean. Simple. Yet risky. Cops were getting smarter with their tracing ability. I couldn't risk them finding out about me and my line of work. Plus, knowing Connor, he had the police on his payroll.

"Are you my airport passenger?" the cabbie asked about ten minutes later as he pulled up beside me. The trail to the opposite side of the cabin didn't take nearly as long as I'd thought.

"I am."

I got in the back of the tan Honda Civic that had a rusty bumper and put the bag in the seat beside me.

"Didn't realize there were any houses out this way," the cabbie said. I noticed the sign on the back side of the driver's side seat that announced my driver as 'Mack.' He looked like a Mack. Salt and pepper beard, trucker hat, and the voice of a chain smoker.

"There isn't," I said without further explanation. "There's an additional hundred-dollar bill with your name on it if you can make it to the airport in under an hour."

"You got it," Mack said. He pulled onto the road, taking the hint that his passenger was not going to be chatty.

Mack earned his hundred-dollar bill by getting me to the airport in forty minutes flat. I made it through security with no issues, but I couldn't help but wonder if Connor had a goon tracking my movements. I had to keep my wits about me, just in case. Amanda was counting on me. I wouldn't fail her again.

AMANDA

Things were not going how I'd hoped. As I sat in the car, unmoving from the last command Connor had given me, I couldn't help but wonder where I'd gone wrong. He'd certainly gotten off from the blow job I'd given him. A tactic I had hoped would stall him from wanting to fuck me. I was terrified that when he tried, I might not be wet for him. And if I wasn't ready, that might be the end of me. It was easier for me to close my eyes and imagine I was sucking off Malcolm. At the same time, Connor's scent was different. Even his energy was menacing, so I could never fully take myself out of the moment. The one saving grace was how fast Connor came. And maybe that's why he was upset with me. He hated losing control. Hated relinquishing power. Even for a moment. Maybe he was putting me back in my place.

"Put this on," Connor said. He handed me his jacket. It dawned on me that walking a woman into a building with nothing but a thin T-shirt would certainly raise a few eyebrows. Something he wouldn't want. I slipped my arms inside the large coat.

When the SUV came to a stop in front of Luxx Apartments & Condos, I had to force myself not to hyperventilate. I couldn't believe I was willingly coming back here. I had to fight every single urge I had not to run the second the car door was opened.

Not that I would have gotten far. Connor's hand was around mine like a Vise-Grip, as though he, too, realized I might try to run.

I gave him a smile to ease his worry. "Shall I follow you?" I asked the question like a well-trained good girl.

"Yes. Amanda. Do not leave my side."

I squeezed his hand back in affirmation. The gesture seemed to shock him, as his eyes darted quickly down at our intertwined hands before they lifted back up to me. With one strong motion, he yanked my arm so that my whole body slid across the seat until I was snug against his side.

"This close. Understood?" he said. His voice was husky.

My lips parted on their own as I nodded my consent.

He lifted me out of the vehicle with ease and set me down right beside him. I pressed my body to his side as his fingers held onto me like a bear trap.

His grip didn't lessen as we went inside. Memories of the first time I walked into this building wafted over me. That poor version of me who did not know the unsuspecting horrors that would greet me a few floors up. And just like that first time, Patricia was there. Her eyes widened slightly when she saw me. But then she turned back into the doll she was trained to be and plastered on a smile. She was far more polite than she had ever been the first time we met. And that's when I realized she had been rude to me that day to try and save me. To get me to leave before Connor showed up. If only I had listened to her.

"Has anyone been in or out?" Connor asked Patricia.

"Just Anita, sir."

He nodded. "When did she leave?"

Patricia looked down at a clipboard. "Six o' three this evening, sir."

"Any messages?"

"No. But your father has tried to call out several times. He's rather upset that he keeps getting me instead."

I watched as Connor's eyes pinched in frustration. That told me two things. One, Connor had a landline, but two, even that was set up with a failsafe. Yet another escape route blocked.

"Thanks, Patricia. You can go. Lock up behind you."

Patricia nodded as Connor dragged me toward the elevator.

Back into that steel box. Back to the time when I thought he might be hitting on me. Back when I had no idea how my life would change.

The elevator doors closed as he stared at my ass. "You know, if you hadn't just blown me, I would have bent you over right here. Just as I wanted to the first day we met. Did you know that?" He dug his fingers into my hips and inhaled deeply.

"I did. Your eyes gave you away. You wanted me just as much as I wanted you." It hadn't been a lie. I remembered very well how hot I thought he was. How hot he turned out to be. It was such a confusing memory to be having.

"We'll play later," Connor said. He pressed a kiss on top of my head, and it was all I could do not to throw up. "Right now, I have business to attend to."

The elevator opened and the blood red carpets down the long hallway greeted me. My stomach twisted as I fought back the nausea. Throwing up now would give me away. I swallowed back the bile and pressed my cheek against his chest to keep myself upright as he walked me back into my prison.

When he got to my cage, he scanned his eyes, and the door unlocked. He pressed me against him and kissed me on the head.

"I'll be back for you soon." He pressed his lips to the top of my head once more before he gestured to the door.

With my heart thundering in my chest, I gave him a small nod and willingly went back into my cage.

Hearing the familiar *Thunk. Beep. Beep. Beep* of the locks sliding into place, I leaned against the door and tried not to pass out from hyperventilation.

"Welcome back," a thin voice said.

My ears perked up as my eyes darted to the vent in the kitchen. *Kelli.*

Pushing off the floor, I ran to the kitchen and pressed my stomach to the floor to check on Kelli.

"You're still here," I whispered. I wasn't sure if I was relieved or terrified. There was no saying what fate awaited her once she was sold, but being here wasn't desirable either.

"So are you," Kelli said. Her voice was thin. "Thought you were going to escape, didn't you? But here you are. Ass back in the cage. Just like he wanted."

"I know." I swallowed down the lump in my throat. She'd been counting on me, and I failed.

"Hey, at least you tried. You got further than anyone else has." Through the vent, I saw Kelli lift her hand. Something white caught my eye.

"Oh my god...your finger," I gasped. I'd nearly forgotten about Connor cutting it off as a threat to Malcolm.

"They re-attached it. Full range of motion is expected once things heal and the swelling goes down..." Her voice was devoid of emotion, "You see, I'm not as valuable broken."

"They re-attached it?" I gasped.

"The surgeon was with me in my cage before they cut it," she said. Her voice seemed detached. "Connor told me what they were going to do if your location wasn't shared. I didn't think he'd really do it, though. I thought it was all just a scare tactic." Kelli held up her bandaged hand, examining it. "It wasn't. The second the video was over, the surgeon was bagging my finger up and putting it on ice. They knocked me out and brought me to his office to sew me back together. Can you believe that? He has a fucking surgeon on call. On his payroll." Kelli shook her head.

"Oh my god," was all I could say.

"It gets worse. The surgeon? He is my soon-to-be master. The guy probably had a hard-on the whole time he was stitching me up."

"Jesus," I said.

"The worst part was…I thought if this is the pain I have to go through for Amanda's plan to work, for one of us to be free, then it would be worth it." She let loose a deep sigh. "That's what I get for daring to hope."

"Kelli, I am so sorry. I—"

"Save it, Amanda. I don't want to hear it. I've accepted my fate. It's time you did too."

Kelli stood up and shoved her mattress in front of the grate, effectively shutting off our communication.

CHAPTER NINETEEN

CONNOR

With Amanda safely back in her cage, I went to my unit and let loose a slight sigh before opening the door. I was dreading the conversation about to come. My father would not have been pleased to be locked inside and would likely be crawling out of his skin at not having a bottle to numb his thoughts.

The retinal scan pulled up the cameras inside. He was sitting on my bed, still alive. The rest of my unit, however, looked like a hurricane had come through. There was debris everywhere.

"What the fuck?" I undid the locks and opened the door, scanning the bits of paper and torn up pillows. Every cabinet in the kitchen was open, the contents inside thrown about in disarray.

"Connie?" came a voice.

"Yeah, it's me, Dad. What the fuck did you do to my apartment?"

My father walked into the room. His hair was wild. He had on a pair of my sweatpants and one of my hoodies, and looked very much strung out. Which made sense. I'd forced him in here without any booze for a few days. Probably the longest stretch he'd ever gone without it.

"You locked me in here! What type of son locks his father on the top of a thirteen-floor apartment with no escape? What if there had been a fire? I could have died!"

"You would have been fine, Dad. There is a sprinkler system," I said calmly. I went over to the couch to move some of the tossed contents of my apartment from the seat so I could sit down. "Why did you tear my house apart?"

"I was looking for a key or a phone."

"You were looking for booze."

My dad lowered his head. It was all the confirmation I needed. Pressing my hand to my forehead to rub away the mounting headache, I gestured to the couch, trying to encourage him to sit, but he shook his head.

"Let me out of here, Connie. You let me out right this second.

"I can't do that yet. Not until I've eliminated the threat."

"Threat? What threat? Look, I know Micky talks a big game if his bookies aren't paid, but he knows not to mess with me. He knows I'm good for it."

"Micky knows not to mess with *me*. Don't delude yourself into thinking he has any respect for you," I clarified. "Micky is the least of my problems. I have an enemy and until they are taken out, you need to be kept safe."

My father's eyes softened. "Aw, Connie, I didn't know you cared so much about your old man."

"Firstly, stop calling me Connie. I'm not a child anymore."

He held up his hands. "No. You're right. I'm sorry." He let loose a slow breath. "I'm sorry about a lot of things, kid."

I raised an eyebrow. "I highly doubt you're sorry for anything you've done."

The bottom lip of his father's mouth quivered. "You're wrong, son. I know I was a shit father." Tears seemed to be welling. "I should have gotten us out of there. Away from your mother."

"So, you did know," I said, finally getting the confirmation I didn't want. "You knew what she was doing to me. You saw it and you did nothing." I shook my head. "Father of the Year."

He said nothing. There was nothing he could say to make up

for any of it. Better to let him sit in his guilt. Still, I didn't want him to think of me as weak for enduring such hell.

"Although, without her teachings, I wouldn't be where I am today. I didn't know it then, but there was so much I had to learn."

"Learn?" he asked. "What could a kid possibly learn from being locked in a cage for days on end without food or water?"

I lifted my hands and gestured around my apartment. "How to effectively cage others." My dad stared at me almost like he couldn't tell if I was pulling his leg or not. Cocking my head to the side, I glared at my father. "It wasn't a joke. Dad, come on. Think about it. How do you think I make a living?"

He shrugged. "You run an adoption agency. You find dogs and get them into a good home."

I couldn't help but smile. "I do indeed. But I don't sell dogs. I sell bitches."

"Ah, so you're a breeder. I wondered how you made so much money on dogs. What breed?"

Leaning forward I watched his expression closely. "No, Dad. I'm not a breeder. I sell women. To horny men. To use and abuse for their sexual deviancy. For the highest price."

"Connor, that's not funny. You shouldn't joke about something like that." I watched as my father took a small step away from me.

"I'm not joking. This whole floor is lined with cages of women ready to sell. This is a billion-dollar business. Thanks to Mother's lessons, I learned how to cage a human and how long they can go without food or water. The mental toll something like that takes. All skills I learned because you did nothing." I walked over to my dad and looked him dead in the eyes. "How to disassociate from the cruelty of my actions? Well, that I learned from my father."

At that moment, it registered. My dad saw me for the monster I was. For his part in creating it.

"Now, if you say a word to *anyone* about what I do, ever, I will find out, and I'll provide you with your own little cage. And maybe this time I'll experiment to see what happens when no food and water is given. Are we quite clear? Not a single person."

My father nodded once but didn't say anything. I think he might have been too stunned to speak. It was time he understood the circles I worked in. Maybe then he'd get his act together.

"So, those cries I heard earlier...that wasn't televisions?" my dad whispered, pointing at the door. "That was the woman you have trapped?" His face was pale.

"Now you're getting it," I said with a small laugh. Then my eyes narrowed, and my tone became lethal. "How else do you think your gambling debts are paid down so quickly? Or how your rent is covered every year. How you want for nothing? Your monthly liquor habit alone is worth the cost of one of those women, so don't sit there and give me that judgmental look. You reap the reward of my lifestyle. You're no better than me."

He gave me a disapproving look before he slumped his shoulders and turned around to go back to my bedroom. This shared living arrangement was not going to work. I needed to find Malcolm and remove the threat or throw my father in an empty cage. While I had three empty cages, that would change soon. Vincent had a load coming in next week, so I needed to make sure the rooms were ready. Daddy Dearest taking up that real estate just wasn't an option.

Before dealing with him, however, I needed to check on the pets and make sure Kelli was ready for her sale. Because of the whole finger debacle, I needed to release her to her surgeon buyer sooner than I'd like. He was worried about infection and wanted to monitor her care. Her new owner was all too eager to take her sooner. Small miracle. Not to mention Anita would be wanting her funds as well for feeding the pets while I was away, but before I gave her payment, I'd need to check her work.

I made my way over to the kitchen and grabbed a few protein bars from off the floor. At least he didn't destroy the food supply in his hunt for a buzz. I was too tired to do much else for them. I just needed them breathing. I didn't need them happy.

With three bars in my hand, I left the unit and locked my father back in. Walking down the hall to Belinda's cage, I pulled up her screens. She was sitting on the floor next to her bed, rocking back and forth. I pressed the intercom and said the only German words I knew.

"*Stuhl. Jetzt!*"

Belinda's eyes darted up, but she quickly got up from the mattress and went to sit in her chair, legs crossed. Good girl.

Unlocking her cage, I stepped inside and let it fall shut behind me.

"Belinda, I think I might have a buyer for you. He is German, so he can at least understand what the fuck you're saying. And he likes the challenge of breaking you in himself, so win-win."

Belinda blinked up at me, completely clueless to what I was telling her.

"I should know by the end of the week. Until then, have a snack." I tossed the bar at her, but she didn't make a move to catch it, so it clocked her on the chin before falling into her lap.

"Not that bright, are you?"

She didn't say anything.

"As you were," I sighed. She was no fun at all. The sooner I offloaded her, the better.

Once she was locked up, I walked past the row of empty cages and approached Kelli's door. Garrett had given me oxy for her pain and had her on a course of antibiotics. The oxy I kept. Keeping the infection at bay was one thing, but I wasn't risking an OD by putting her on oxy. She'd suffer through the pain like everyone else in the world had to.

Tending to her wound was yet another fucking annoyance. And I blamed Malcolm for this one. I couldn't wait for the day that it would be his dick that I cut off.

AMANDA

Walking slowly around the room, I did my best to keep my face neutral. No trace of fear or panic could be revealed. I was on camera and knew he was recording my every move. I only prayed he wouldn't make out the conversation I'd had with Kelli. We'd kept our voices barely above a whisper, but even so, I'd have to be far more careful than that or Connor would see right through my act.

That's when I heard the sound of someone's cage being opened down the hall. It didn't sound like it was close, so it probably wasn't Kelli's. While I wanted to rush over to the door and press my ear to it to try and figure out what was happening, instead, I sat down on the fucking red wingback chair and crossed my ankles, hands on the armrests, and waited like the good pet he expected me to be.

I sat in that damn chair for what had to be over an hour, but he never came into my room. I wasn't sure if that was good or bad. When it became clear that Connor wasn't going to show, I got up from the chair and went over to the mattress. Sinking myself onto the cold, sheetless bed, my body recoiled at the thought of sleeping in this room once again.

Hugging my arms across my body, I held onto one thought: *At least I was able to save Malcolm.* It was the only bit of hope holding me together. As long as Connor or his men didn't find him, this would all have been worth it.

Exhaustion took over at some point and I fell asleep. When I awoke it was to an oddly familiar scent.

Bacon and coffee. The same smells I'd encountered the first night I had been locked in my cell. And, as before, when I opened my eyes, Connor was there holding a paper plate with scrambled eggs, two slices of bacon, and half a slice of toast. I nearly hurled from the memory.

"Morning," Connor said. He placed the plate on the bed beside me, which had no utensils. I still hadn't earned those. I was starting at ground zero.

"You made me breakfast?" I sat up and rubbed the sleep from my eyes.

"It's day one protocol. Give the pets something familiar. Lull them into a false sense of safety." He smiled. "Teach them that what can be given, can always be taken away."

I nodded, trying not to show how horrified I was. I picked up a slice of bacon, but before I could place it in my mouth, his hand was around my wrist. "I didn't give you permission to eat."

Fuck. I'd messed up already. I dropped the bacon, and it fell onto my lap. Connor didn't release my hand as he reached down and picked up the bacon from off my thigh. He held it up to my lips, dragging it slowly over them. "You are like this bacon to me, Amanda. Delicious and salty. But very dangerous for my heart." He took a large bite out of the bacon as his hand held my chin in place. Using his thumb, he forced my mouth open. "Because you're so dangerous, I have to be careful when I eat you. Do you understand?"

I nodded as best I could in the grip he had on my skull. He held me there, my mouth locked open as he slowly chewed the bit of bacon. After a moment, he tossed the half slice back onto the plate and he let me go.

"What do I mean, Amanda?"

My heart sped up. I only had one shot at giving the answer he wanted. I swallowed once to wet my mouth "You mean that as much as you might want to fuck me, you can't trust me yet."

Connor's eyes narrowed. "Very astute. I knew you were smarter than your body gave you credit for." He stood up and looked down at me sitting on the bed. "You haven't been fully housebroken. So no, I can't trust you yet. But that's not your fault. Your training had only begun when you were stolen from me."

"Will you train me now?" I asked.

"That's not the right question," Connor said. "The right

question is which method do I train you with? As a foster pet, or as *my* pet. Two very different protocols."

The gasp of shock surprised us both.

"Is this news upsetting to you? I thought you wanted to be my pet," Connor said as the thin lines around his eyes tightened.

I cursed at myself for letting my guard down. I had to come up with a reason for the look of horror on my face. "It's nothing, it's just...I thought you told me you'd never had a pet before. But if you have a pet training protocol, then it means you have, so..."

Connor stared at me for a moment before he smiled. "Is this jealousy I hear in your voice?"

I lowered my head, trying to look wounded.

"I have never owned a pet before. Far too dangerous. But if I ever did have one, there is a very specific way in which I would teach them."

"Which is?" I asked.

Connor stared at me and I couldn't help but wonder if I'd messed up again.

"If I decide to keep you, you'll find out. In the meantime, eat."

He pointed at the food beside me as he backed up to the wall to watch me. Having no choice, I did as I was told. I started with the bit of bacon he had half eaten. I brought it to my lips slowly, sliding the crispy meat inside my mouth as sensually as I could. It was hard not to gag as the bacon hit the back of my throat, but I could tell my choice to eat the bacon first pleased him. Finally, I had done something right.

He watched me like a hawk as I ate every bit of food. Our eyes locked the entire time. Once I had finished the meal, he took the empty paper plate and paper cup in his hand.

His eyes narrowed as they raked over me. I held my breath afraid the fear would be overheard. His lip twitched, and I wondered if he was going to throw me onto the bed and take me right now, but instead, he took a step backward.

"I know what you're doing," he said.

"What I'm doing?" I asked, trying to come off seductive and not terrified that the jig was up.

He smirked and went to the bedroom door. "You want me to fuck you. And I will. All in good time. I don't have time to play today. Lots of fires to put out. But don't worry, I'll be making up for lost time soon. Until then, think about all the ways I'm going to make you come."

I sucked in a breath and held back a shiver. My reaction seemed to please him because he turned on his heel and then left me without another word. I couldn't tell if I'd passed some test or if I'd pissed him off. It was hard to know with Connor. I was a pawn in a game I didn't fully understand. And that was exactly the way he wanted it. Trapped physically and mentally.

CHAPTER TWENTY
Malcolm

Even with a direct flight across the country, I was still in the air for five hours. Five hours I was helpless to do anything about Amanda's situation. All I could think about was what he might be doing to her. In what ways might Connor be punishing or torturing her for daring to leave him?

What if he didn't bring her back to where he originally held her? What if he had safehouses too? What then?

The second I was off the plane and in the rental, I was on the phone with Darcy.

"Any updates? Do you know if he brought her back to the Luxx building?"

Darcy let loose a deep sigh. "Unconfirmed. We found some traffic camera footage that shows Connor arriving with a woman with short black hair, wearing what looked like his suit jacket, but we didn't get a good look at her face."

Malcolm rubbed his temple. "It's her. She dyed her hair while we were on the run. How did she look?"

"It was hard to see. It was like two seconds of footage."

"And no sign that he's taken her back out?"

"Not that we've seen."

Which meant that he'd put her back in her cage. Anger boiled over my skin. I had to do something, but what? I was coming up blank.

"Status on the safehouse?" I asked, stalling for time.

"It's been reduced to ash, which is not a bad thing. Your dummy holdings will cover the damages."

"And the vehicles?"

Darcy's tone picked up. "This is the best part. So, it turns out that Kenny guy that Connor took out? He has a bunch of warrants out for his arrest. And Hodge, as you know, was a bounty hunter when he wasn't working for us, so the cops have already pinned Hodge's death on Kenny. According to a press conference, they assume they took each other out so that trail should end there."

"That is a logical conclusion. Far more believable than the truth."

"Exactly," Darcy said. "It will be in their news cycles for a few weeks, but once everyone gets paid for their cleanup work, the dust will settle."

"I'm still down a house though." I sighed. It was my favorite of them because of the connection it had with my mother.

"I know. But what matters is that you're safe. No signs you were followed?" she asked.

I shook my head subconsciously but checked my rearview mirror for the hundredth time before responding. "Not that I've seen."

"Well, that's good. Which house do you want me to have opened up for you? Your Seattle condo or the Portland house?"

"Neither."

"Oh. Where will you go then?" Darcy asked.

"The only place I can go. Luxx Apartments & Condos."

"Malcolm, don't be stupid. You can't face off with Connor. He'll—"

"Not if I kill him first."

I hung up the phone and tossed it on the front seat. It was time to end this once and for all.

Pulling up my GPS, I plugged in the coordinates for the

nearest hardware store. My years as a Boy Scout were about to come in handy. Or get me killed. One of the two.

As I was walking down one of the aisles in the store, I got a text from Camila.

> A car just came to your house. Some thug got out and walked up to one of the security cameras to deliver a message.

> What did they say?

> Not a word. He just held up a picture. He's trying to get under your skin. Don't let him. Sending now.

I waited impatiently for the image to load. I braced myself for another chopped finger but instead, I saw a picture of what looked like the inside of a vehicle. Of course he'd have surveillance cameras everywhere. The camera was focused on the back seat of the car. There was no mistaking what I was looking at. Amanda was on her knees in the car, giving Connor head. One word of text was over the image. "Mine."

"That sick fuck." I quickly deleted the image. I never needed to see it again. It was permanently burned in my brain.

> I'm going dark. You two stay hidden.

I typed, then powered down the phone.

I was going to put an end to this. An end to Connor. But first, I would make him pay for forcing Amanda to do his bidding. I refused to believe she'd willingly gone down on him. Unless it was a strategy. A way to get him to trust her. Fuck. That's probably exactly what she'd done. She was making him believe she loved him. As much as I hated that she had to do that, it was a strong survival tactic. And the very thing I told her to do if he caught her. Pretend to love him. However, I wasn't sure how long she'd be able to keep up the ruse. Which was why I needed to intervene. Now.

"Can I help you find something?" A college-age kid asked as he approached me inside the store. He was hard to miss in his neon work apron.

"Yeah, do you have a store flyer?"

"They're at the front of the store, sir."

"Perfect. Also, do you sell steel wool?"

"We do." He gestured behind him. "Follow me. I'll show you where we keep it."

Step one: Gather the supplies needed to hunt the monster. Step two: Don't die in the attempt. That was it. That was the whole plan. It wasn't much, but it was simple. It just relied on everything working perfectly from this point forward.

CONNOR

After locking Amanda up, I leaned my head against the outside of her door. It was so hard walking away from her. I wanted to throw her down and have her in so many ways. She wanted it too, but I had to be smart. I had to get my business affairs straight. Then I had to get my father into a safe location other than my fucking place, but mostly, I had to find and kill Malcolm. That's when I could have Amanda in all of the carnal ways I needed to have her. *Priorities, Connor.*

Bypassing my apartment, I took the trash to the lobby and dumped it in one garbage bin before making my way to the office.

Once inside, I picked up the phone and called Gwen's buyer as agreed. He was, naturally, concerned with her finger. Even though he did the surgical work himself, it wasn't done under the best circumstances.

"Evening, Garrett. It's Brooks. Calling with an update on your adoption if you have a moment."

"Just a sec." The sound of the phone shuffled and then there was a "'click'" of a door closing. "Okay, go ahead."

"I just checked on her 'paw.' There is still some swelling and discomfort, but no signs of infection. Patricia told me you might want to move up the adoption date so you can monitor her healing on your own?"

"I think that's only appropriate, given the circumstances in which her 'paw' was injured. I also think it's appropriate that her adoption fee be significantly reduced."

I was waiting for that. Garrett was well within his rights to ask for a discount. After all, I was selling him damaged goods. Even if she regained full function in her finger as he said she would, providing things healed properly, she would always have the scar. Still...

"Oh, I don't know, Garrett. I'm thinking this bitch might have learned who her master was in this instance. Which will make your training at home so much easier. A mere reminder of the paw injury would be enough to keep her in line for years to come. Wouldn't you agree?"

"I want a ten percent discount and want her delivered by the end of the day or the adoption is off."

I brought my hand up to the bridge of my nose and squeezed. Normally, I wouldn't entertain this counteroffer, but I certainly didn't have the mental energy to deal with a broken pet. If I offloaded her now, I could stick my dad in her cage and still have room for the others coming in on the first of the month. If anything, Garrett was helping me.

"Of course. As you wish. Are we dropping her at the same location as was listed in your adoption papers?" I pulled up his file on my computer to see he had a back entrance to his surgical office listed for the drop off.

"Yes, that's fine.

"Consider it done." I shot a text to the boys for retrieval. "And might I just say, you picked out the perfect collar for her? She won't be breaking out of your backyard with that shock collar on."

Garrett had taken me up on my advice to put up the electric fence around his premises. It was always advisable with new adoptions until the flight risk dissipated. Usually, around six months after they had succumbed to their new master. With the collar on, it would drop them in two seconds if they even came close to the fence.

"End of the day, Brooks." Garrett hung up on me.

Normally, I'd be pissed, but I wasn't. One headache tended to. Belinda should be offloaded next week, freeing up the floor for the next group of apartment hunters coming in a few days. That's how the adoption business was. Sometimes the floor stood empty for months, while other times it was overflowing.

Which was why my next call was to Vincent. While I found most of my own pets through my fake rental ads, Vincent and I would occasionally sell our pets to each other when one of us got in a larger-than-planned haul.

"Brooks," Vincent said once he finally picked up. "Still have a pet you need to offload?"

"Actually, about that. Wondering if I might get something else from you instead."

"What do you need?"

"I'll text you the specs. The closest you can get would be fine."

I quickly typed the details and hit send.

"Ah... Yeah, I got something like that," Vincent said. "Right in your neck of the woods as a matter of fact. Could have it to ya in a few hours. That work?"

"I'll pay you double if you can. And Vincent, discreet packaging, yeah?"

"This ain't my first rodeo, kid. Anything else?"

"That's all for now."

We hung up and I sighed. I'd made a huge decision during that call, and I hadn't even realized it until now. The path on what to do with Amanda had been made.

Once Gwen was moved later, I'd stash my dad in her cage, and Amanda could be moved into my apartment, with Vincent's addition. With both of those safeguards in place, I'd have the time to pursue Malcolm full force and still keep a close eye on Amanda.

Which reminded me, I needed to check on Malcolm's tail. Making a final call, I reached out to the team leader.

"What's the update?" I asked the second Eric picked up.

"We scattered. Too many eyes around with the blaze. Tony and his group went to Vermont to await instructions. I'm here in Maine, about an hour away waiting to see what you wanted us to do."

"What do you mean scattered? You lost him?"

"There were cops and fire crews everywhere, Boss. We had to lay low or we'd be questioned. By the time we got here, the place was ash. If he was inside, he is toast."

"He wasn't inside, you moron. He was out in the woods somewhere. He probably clocked your asses and ran." I let loose a breath to contain my rage. "What's done is done. I need you to get back on the scent. He's likely flown from there already, but check airline rosters and bus schedules. Find out where he went. He would probably be in a hurry and thus make mistakes in his escape."

"You got it."

"Eric, if you don't find Malcolm, none of you get paid. You know this, right?"

"We know the terms. We'll find him."

"You better."

CHAPTER TWENTY-ONE
Amanda

Connor didn't return to my unit for the rest of the day. Not even for a food drop. Not that I had any appetite, but it did seem odd that he'd let us go without food. I tried several times to talk to Kelli, but she refused to say anything to me. It was like she'd shut herself down. I couldn't blame her. If her hunch was right, and she was about to be sold off to the butcher who sewed her back up, I would become numb to everything too.

That's when I heard through the intercom the order to "sit in the chair." I nearly jumped out of my skin but quickly plastered on a smile, knowing that he was watching. I rushed over to the red wingback, sat with my ankles crossed, arms on the armrests, and waited for my captor. Something told me this would be the moment I was going to have to put up or shut up. Convince him I loved him or be sold off like Kelli. Or worse.

Thunk. Beep. Beep. Beep.

My cage was unlocked.

The door opened slowly. Connor stood there, a devilish grin on his face. "Such a well behaved girl. So good, I've bought you a present."

"A present?" I asked, hoping for a blanket or even some pants.

Instead, Connor shoved into the unit a large box. The outside of the box boasted that it was a forty-three-inch smart TV. A happy family in the corner of the box was pointing at the cinematic wonder on the mounted screen.

"It's not what it looks like," Connor said. Leaning the box against the wall, he locked the door. "It's how Vincent ships his packages."

Vincent. That was the name of the other human trafficker that Connor had threatened to sell me to. He kept his women in literal dog kennels. The TV box was too narrow for such a thing, thankfully.

Connor broke the taped seal of the box and slowly pulled out something large and metal. The sound of it scraping against the hardwood floors sent chills down my spine.

I sat in the chair, trying to slow my heart as I watched him pull at the long sides of the metal, popping up a panel at a time until it became clear what had been folded up inside that harmless-looking TV box.

It *was* a kennel. A collapsible one. Except this one was all metal with only small quarter-sized holes drilled into the top few inches for breathing. The rest of it was solid sheet metal.

"What is it?" I heard myself ask, trying to keep the fear from my voice.

"Come now, Amanda, you know exactly what this is." He opened the kennel door. The metallic squeak of the hinges turned my insides to ice.

"You're selling me to Vincent," I whispered.

Connor smirked. "That's not out of the question. But no, it's not the current plan."

"What is the plan then?"

Connor came over to the chair and took my wrists, pulling me upwards. When our bodies were pressed together, he looked at the cage.

"The plan is that I train you to be my pet. I told you the training would be different if I decided to keep you."

"You're going to keep me?" I tried to sound excited and not terrified.

"If you can survive the training, yes."

"What do I have to do?"

His eyes darted to the kennel. "You'll be trained to obey the way I was when I was a boy. I will teach you the same lesson that I had to learn. Submission. Complete and utter submission. To accept whatever conditions I demand," he said, running his finger across my chin. "It's the only way I can know for sure if I can keep you as a pet. As *my* pet. There has to be no question in my mind that you will do my bidding at every moment. No matter how vile my commands may be."

I felt my heart race. "Oh," I whispered. My eyes darted to the kennel. "How long will I need to be inside?"

"As long as I fucking want you to be." He cupped my ass firmly. His erection pressed into me.

I gasped, feeling him this close. I knew this was all part of my effort to save Malcolm's life, but now I was having serious doubts about how sound of a plan it was.

That's when I felt Connor's hands tugging off my shirt, leaving me in just my underwear. I fought my instincts to cover myself up. I let him look at me and forced the panic to stay off my face.

"Get in the cage, Amanda."

His order was quiet. Simple. And the most terrifying I'd ever heard him.

Swallowing the lump in my throat, I approached the cage. Because it was so small, I had to get on my hands and knees. My palms hit the cold metal and my skin goosefleshed. Nausea swept over me.

"Keep going," he ordered.

I forced my body inside. There was no room to move or even stretch my legs. I was on my hands and knees, with my nose practically touching the metal wall in the back.

"Good girl," he said. Shutting the door behind me, my reality started to seep in. A padlock clicked into place and instantly, I started to panic. It was one thing to be put inside. A whole different level of fear hearing a lock being put on. There was nowhere to move. No escape.

"That's just where I want you. On your knees, waiting for my command." He moved from behind the cage and walked around to the front. Through the air holes, I saw him stand by my door. I could only see him from the waist up, but it was enough to see what he was doing.

Leaning against my door, he undid his belt. Unbuttoned his pants and took down his fly. With little effort, his pants fell to the floor as he held his cock in his hand.

"This is step one, Amanda. If you truly want to be my pet...this is where your training starts. Do you understand?" he asked as he worked his hand up and down his length. "As my pet, you will be used for my pleasure and my pleasure alone."

As much as I wanted to look away from what Connor was doing, I knew it would be worse if I did. He wanted me to observe him. After all, this was what I had wanted. What I'd begged him for. Back when I thought this was the only way out of a worse fate. I was a fool.

A few pumps later and he came all over the cage. I could hear it landing on the top of the metal like rain on a rooftop. He panted against the wall for a few minutes as his cock twitched and relaxed before he pulled his pants back up.

After a moment, he sighed. "Sleep well, my pet."

My eyes widened realizing he was going to be leaving me in this metal box overnight.

"Connor. No. Please, you can't leave me in here. I'll be good. I'll do anything you want me to—" I tried.

"I know you will. And what I want is for you to stay in this fucking cage until I decide to take you out. Understood?"

The edge in his voice was lethal. I'd already fucked up. I nodded and swallowed my fear.

"Yes, Connor."

"At least you don't have to try and sleep on metal bars like I had to. The sheet metal will be much nicer to your knees. Trying to stay asleep while laying in your own excrement, though, you never really get used to that one." He smiled wickedly. "Goodnight, pet."

MALCOLM

One of the advantages I had over Connor was that I used to own the building where he was currently running his operations. Another was that I had a working relationship with the adjacent building's maintenance manager. A building that had a shared electrical room that only C.J. and the power company had access to.

Since I knew Connor would have cameras watching the outside of his property, I couldn't just waltz up to C.J. and ask him to let me bust into Connor's electrical room. So I did the next best thing. I found C.J. at the pub. His home away from home.

"Well, well, well. Look what the cat dragged in." C.J. looked exactly like you'd picture a maintenance worker. Dark blue coveralls, a white tank top, with a thick gold chain around his neck, and thinning gray hair slicked back to within an inch of its life. He took a pull from his cigarette and blew the smoke over his shoulder.

"I thought you couldn't smoke in pubs anymore?" I wafted the smoke away.

"You can't," C.J. said. "But I'm special." He took one last drag of his butt before he put it out on the bottom of his shoe.

"I ain't seen you around this neck of the woods in a minute. You slummin' it?" C.J. asked, patting the stool beside him. The bar was all but empty this time of day, which was perfect for the conversation I wanted to have with him.

"I need a favor." I shifted in my seat. No sense beating around the bush when it came to C.J.

"Figured as much. Transport?"

I shook my head. C.J.'s repair van came in handy when moving larger paintings in and out of locations.

"Something a bit more challenging."

C.J. lifted a bushy graying eyebrow. "What kind of challenge are we talking about?"

I lowered my voice. I didn't need a nosy bartender overhearing our conversation. "I need access to the electrical box at Luxx."

"Do I want to know why?"

"Probably safer if you don't," I said.

C.J. merely nodded. "And what's in it for me?"

I let loose a breath. I knew there was one thing I had that C.J. wanted that I vowed I would never let go of. "*The Amateur*," I sighed. "The original. Not a print."

"Jesus," C.J. whispered. While C.J. wasn't a big art fan, his daughter, Sophia, was an art dealer. And she had coveted my first commissioned work since she started her own gallery. I'd sold the original years ago, then broke into the new owner's home and replaced it with a copy. Even a trained eye would have a hard time knowing the difference between the two. It was currently valued at over two hundred and three million dollars. Which is why I wanted it for myself. It was the ultimate backup plan.

"What exactly do you need access to?" C.J. asked. The fact that he was even considering the deal made me relax.

"Let's take a walk. To your building," I said.

C.J. nodded, reaching into his pocket to grab some cash for his unfinished drink.

Twenty minutes later, we were in the basement adjoining the two properties. One electrical room with a large, locked metal door stood between them.

"What do you need me to do?" C.J. asked.

"How much do you know about what goes on in my old building?"

C.J. shrugs. "Not much of anything that I can see. It's still under renovation."

"That's what he wants you to see. The less you know what's

really going on the better, just trust me that it's vile. I need you to kill the electricity for...maybe thirty minutes. Can you do that?"

"Well, yeah, but that won't do much. There's a generator system—"

"A generator system that I bought and paid for. Unless he's changed it, which I doubt, the system is designed for powering on only the most important areas. So things like the elevator, hall lights, and exit areas. Emergency access situations."

"Yeah, sure. Makes sense. Let me guess. What you need access to isn't one of those areas?"

"Bingo. He'll be so flustered about why his systems are off that he won't be looking in the back alley. Hell, I doubt he ever replaced the faulty wiring in the camera back there."

"Camera? Like a security camera?"

I nodded. "My line of work is not exactly on the right side of the law, as you are well aware. And Connor's definitely isn't. But when I owned the building, I needed a way to get my stuff safely from place to place. I'd put things in a garbage bag and make my way to the back-alley dumpsters, but I'd go into the back-alley entrance instead."

"Huh. I didn't know there was an entrance back there."

"No one does. It's hidden. Under a manhole cover." I flinched. I shouldn't have told him that much. "It doesn't matter. The thing I need help with is cutting the power so I can get in undetected."

"In exchange for the painting?"

"Yes."

"What will you do once you're inside?" C.J. asked as he rattled his keychain.

"If all goes well, save a life." *And end one.*

CHAPTER TWENTY-TWO

Connor

I didn't even bother to lock Amanda's unit. There wasn't any need. She wasn't going anywhere. In fact, I left the door open. I wanted her to see how close she was to being free of her cage but knowing...submitting to the knowledge that she was where I wanted her. The sooner she accepted her place under my thumb, the better. Once she did that, then I could truly take her on as my pet. Until then, many caged weeks were ahead of her. Which was good. I needed the time to focus on business. I'd been away from it for too long. There was sure to be some fire I'd need to put out somewhere. Then there was my father I still had to deal with. Nightmare.

That's when the elevator doors opened. I instinctively reached for my gun, relaxing only when I saw it was Carlos and one of his men.

"Something wrong, boys?" I asked, easing my finger off the trigger.

"It's three o'clock."

"And?" I asked, annoyed beyond belief.

"That's when you told us to be here. The transfer day for 'Gwen'? We got a truck downstairs that just showed for the pick up."

"Fuck. Gwen. Right. Right. God damn it. The hours have run away on me."

"What kennel is it? Is it that one?" The guy I didn't know asked as he took a step toward Amanda's room. My gun was out and pressed to the dude's neck faster than he had time to even register what was happening.

"Fucking touch anything in that room and it will be the last thing you do."

The guy's eyes were wide as he lifted his hands in surrender. "Sure thing. You got it."

"Who the fuck is this?" I asked Carlos, keeping my weapon locked on the jugular of my target. The dude couldn't be more than twenty-five. Maybe thirty. Built, scurfy stubble, scar across his left eyebrow. I'd never seen him before. And I knew everyone in the business.

"Name's Holden. He's one of Vincent's guys," Carlos said. I lifted the gun from his neck, never taking my eyes off him. While he looked like he could bench two of me on a bad day, there was something soft about him. He cowered like a puppy when death was threatened, which told me he at least had a survival instinct. Holden wore a thick silver necklace and had some sort of tattoo poking over the neckline of his shirt, a shirt that was almost bursting from the strain against his muscles. He might be tough as fuck, but he knew who the alpha was.

"Well, Holden, I don't fucking know you."

Holden looked at me, then at Carlos, as though he wasn't sure if he was allowed to speak. He wasn't.

"Vincent found him in Mexico last year," Carlos offered.

"If he's one of Vincent's men, why is he in my building?"

"We were short a guy now that Kenny... I asked Vincent if we could use one of his men for the day. Holden was up this way already after a transfer, so we got him."

So it was my fault there was a new guy. Still, I didn't know if I trusted this Holden kid yet. "Tell me, Holden, what was a white boy like you doing in Mexico?"

"Ex-military, sir. Dishonorably discharged," he said.

"For what?"

Holden's eyes darted to the floor. "Indecent conduct with a minor, sir. She told me she was nineteen. Turns out she wasn't."

"Well, *Holden*, the military might have dishonorably discharged you for such indiscretions, but if you lay an inappropriate hand on any of *my* women, your job won't be the only thing you lose. Do we understand each other?"

"Completely. Your reputation precedes you, sir," Holden said. His voice had the level of intimidation someone like me warranted.

I turned back to Carlos. "You trust this guy?"

"No problems yet. Knows his place."

I glared at Holden. "He better. Or I'll chop off your cock too."

Carlos nodded as Holden subtly covered his package with his hands. That was the right response.

"So, we clear to move her?" Carlos asked once the tension was cut.

"Yeah. Yeah. This is good actually. I needed the space. You got a case for her?"

"It's by the loading dock."

"Perfect. Let me get her roofied and her take-home bag. Back in a second. Touch nothing." I headed toward my unit.

Inside, my dad was sitting on the couch, his eyes focused on nothing. I would have assumed he was drunk, but I knew that was impossible.

"The fuck's your problem?" I asked as I walked past him to my bedroom.

"My problem? My *problem?*" he shouted from the next room. A second later he was standing in the doorframe. "My problem, Son, is that I've been kidnapped. As have the women you've got locked up in here. My problem is that my son is a psychopath!"

"I'm a *sociopath*, Dad. Get it right. And I'll give you two guesses about where I learned that behavior from. Now shut the fuck up. I have work to do."

"She'd be proud of you," he said after a minute. "Your mother. She'd be proud of the man you've become. That thought alone should be enough to make your skin crawl."

I paused in midreach of grabbing Gwen's bag with her collar in it.

"The whole time I was with your mother, she only ever cared about one thing: how much money we had. It was never enough. Money was the only way to earn her respect. Why do you think I gambled so much? Why I still do. Even after all these years, I'm still trying to earn her approval. Guess I should have been smart like you and gone the human trafficking route, eh?"

"You've never done a smart thing in your life. If you had even a shred of intelligence you would have taken me out of that house when you knew what she was doing to me," I spat. "But you didn't. You did her bidding. So don't spout off to me like you're all high and mighty. You are just as much to blame for the person I turned into."

He was trying to get under my skin. Have me take pity on him, release him. Let him go back to his bottle. And I would. Once Malcolm was dead. One fire at a time.

Unload the pet. Locking my father back in, I went to Gwen's door.

"Sit in your chair, Gwen. It's time to go home."

AMANDA

It was really hard not to lose hope, given my situation. I was naked inside a metal box, inside an even bigger cage. And the worst part? I'd put myself here. And by the conversation happening in the hallway, I hadn't done anything to help Kelli escape this hell either. There was very little hope to cling to. Even my thoughts of Malcolm being safe dwindled by the second. I had no way of knowing if Connor's men had found him and taken him out.

Sucking in a slow breath, I tried my best to disassociate. If I could clock out mentally, then maybe I would survive the night. But then what? How long would he keep me inside this box? How long could my mind hold out? Did I even want to?

That's when I heard Connor's voice in the hallway again.

"Stay here. I need a minute with the transfer," he said. "Once she's under, you can take her to the loading dock. And Carlos, take care with her finger. The buyer will be pissed if she's hurt any more. And if the buyer is pissed, I'm pissed. You don't want that. Just ask Kenny what happens when I lose my temper."

From inside the box, I couldn't see much through the crack in the open door. Just a broad shoulder and a bit of the hallway. I wanted to scream for Kelli to run. To hide. To claw Connor's eyes out with her hands, but all of it would be futile and get us both hurt or killed. All I could do was listen and observe what my fate might play out to if I failed Connor's personal pet training.

"Sit in your chair, Gwen. It's time for you to go home."

I could only imagine what might be going through her mind. Terror, numbness? Maybe relief that this part of the nightmare was over?

"It's your lucky day," Connor was saying. "Your foster wants you now, not in a few more weeks. Your visit during your surgery must have impressed him. He's eager to take care of you himself. Well done." Maybe her new owner would be kinder... It was hard to imagine someone being worse. "When you wake, you'll be in your new home. I trust you understand the consequences of your behavior with your new master?"

Kelli made no noise, as was the smart play.

"If they find you are not compliant or your new foster is unhappy with you for *any* reason, you will be returned to me for additional training. You don't want that. Untrainable pets are put down. Do you understand?" There was the sound of skin being slapped. "Answer me with more than a nod."

"Yes, Master," she said. Her voice was devoid of any emotion. She was on autopilot. That was a blessing.

A few minutes passed before Connor told the men in the hallway to come and claim her.

"Keep me updated, Carlos."

"Oh, Holden will be going with her, sir. I'm on a cargo pickup. That ad you ran for the new building in Canada. We have three trapped there. You wanted me to check on them. Is that not still the plan?"

"Fuck," Connor said. It sounded like he had completely forgotten about that arrangement. But now he had an operation in Canada? How widespread was his business?

"Daily reports, new guy. Daily. You got it? I need to know if she tries to run or disobeys her new owner in any way. For the next two weeks, your ass is parked outside of his place, watching for any escape or police intervention. You got that?"

"Understood, sir. Not my first rodeo."

"Yeah, well, it's your first with me."

"Daily reports, sir."

From my tiny peephole, I saw one of the guys lifting an unconscious Kelli over his shoulder. Then the sound of the elevator rang. And just like that, it was the last time I'd ever see Kelli again. Something inside me felt like it had turned to ice.

"Well, that was exciting. Wasn't it?" Connor's voice was suddenly beside my cage. I jumped, crashing a shoulder against the metal.

"Consider yourself lucky, Amanda. *Gwen* is going to a bit of a sadistic home. Because of his career, her new owner gets off on detaching and re-attaching body parts. You should have seen the boner he had when sewing her finger back up. She'll end up looking like Frankenstein's bride before the year's over. Mark my words." Connor laughed.

He sat and leaned against my cage as my stomach lurched. I felt the box shift slightly as he adjusted his weight. The sigh he let out told me he was exhausted.

"The last few days have been a bit of a shitshow, Amanda, but you're back now." He sighed. "Malcolm will be taken care of any minute now, and now that Gwenny here is gone, my father can stay in her cage until I get confirmation of Malcolm's death. Then... then, Amanda, we can start our fun. Within, I'd say, a week or two, all the loose ends will be taken care of."

"Two weeks?" I heard myself ask. "Inside this box?"

A soft chuckle escaped his lips. "It might be more. I know it seems awful now, but trust me, in time, you'll grow to love being inside your kennel. If you're good, I might even buy you a larger one for my place. Hell, maybe even a dog bed to go inside it. Wouldn't *that* be luxurious?" His fingers knocked against the metal. "Just be grateful your cage has a smooth bottom. Mine didn't. To this day, I still feel the wire bars pressing into my knees."

"Yes, Connor. Thank you," I whispered, holding back my tears. This was it. This was now my reality. The inside of this metal box.

"I know...it's awful now," he said softly. "But it will be worth it. In the end. There is an innate freedom in submitting to your base nature. We've drifted so far away from it as a society. That's why the world is a mess, if you ask me. You'll see. A woman's place is to submit, and a man's is to dominate. That is the true power dynamic. Once that clicks for you...suddenly everything will make sense. I promise."

Connor didn't say anything else, and I wondered if he expected me to say something in return. I opted to keep quiet. To try and sink into the dark corner of this box and pretend that I was anywhere else in the world except here.

That's when he started to snore softly. My unit door was still wide open, and my captor was asleep. And yet I was more trapped than I'd ever been. There was nothing I could do. Nothing except succumb to my fate.

CHAPTER TWENTY-THREE

Malcolm

I looked at the large fuse boxes in front of me as C.J. rubbed his chin. The reality of the plan was still formulating in my mind. Not how I liked to operate. Sure, I was skilled at breaking and entering, but never with someone as smart as Connor. If this plan went wrong, it wasn't just a stint in jail or a large fine, but the end of mine, and possibly Amanda's, life.

"How long can you give me before you flip the power back on?" I asked.

"Well, I figure if I cut the power to just his building, that will look pretty suspect. And I don't need his men on my ass," C.J. said.

"No. No, you don't."

"Best do both buildings then. I'll catch hell from my tenants to fix the problem ASAP, so the most I can give you is maybe thirty minutes. Any longer than that, and they might start calling my higher-up to complain, and I ain't got time for that headache."

"That's plenty of time," I said. And it should be, if everything went according to plan. "One last thing...I need to borrow your gun."

C.J. raised his bushy eyebrows. I knew he would. C.J. had a license to carry a concealed weapon and loved to brag about how no one would mess with him because of it.

"Only has four rounds in it," C.J. said, unzipping his coverall to take the gun from its holster. "If it don't have four when you give it back to me, I don't wanna know about it. Deal?"

"Deal."

"Text me when you're in position."

I nodded and headed through the back of his building to walk the street opposite the entrances. I leaned against the wall by the alley, but well out of the sight of any cameras he might have covering the area.

I'm in position.

A moment later, the text from C.J. came in.

Your clock starts now.

As quickly as possible, I made it into the back alley, opened the manhole cover, and shimmied down the small ladder. Sliding the cover back on took a little more time than I was hoping for, but I couldn't risk anyone wondering why the cover was off and coming to investigate.

Once I was under the buildings, I could hear the hum of the generators that had kicked on. Working my way over to the Luxx side of the building, I listened. Not that I'd be able to hear anything, but I already knew what would be happening. The power would have been cut, then partially restored thanks to the generators I installed. At this point, he'd probably be checking his cameras first. That's what I would do. There wouldn't be anything to see immediately, as the cameras would have gone through a forced reset when switching to generator power. It would take several minutes to get the footage back up, and access to the older footage would have to wait for the restoration of power. The generators would be focused on emergency needs. And backup was not one of them. For now, he would have no idea I was under his building. I intended to keep it that way for as long as I could.

Quickly, I worked my way to the utility room. This was where my plan would either play out perfectly, or I'd have done all this for nothing. It would all come down to this next play.

In retrospect, a lighter would have made my life easier, but I knew if I was discovered and Connor's men found me, they would have taken it anyway. What Connor didn't know about me was that I was a Boy Scout. You didn't need a lighter to start a fire. I took off my shoe and gave it a shake. The single nine-volt battery hiding painfully under my high-arched foot fell into my hand.

A nine-volt battery, when you touched it against steel wool, would create a spark. I took off my other shoe and produced the steel wool pad. And if you happened to have some kindling—I reached into my suit jacket and pulled out the accordion-folded store flyer—then you could make a fire.

I looked up at the sprinkler head a few feet away from the electrical panel and said a little prayer.

The whole plan was, on the surface, a simple one: Start a fire and trigger the sprinkler system. Trip as many as I could from this level. I couldn't set off all the heads in the building, but this, coupled with the power outage, should be enough to make the fire department rush to investigate. And that was the real end game.

Reaching into my pocket, I dialed C.J. "Make the call."

"You sure no one can trace this back to me?" he asked.

"It's a burner. Remember, tell them you saw the fire coming from the thirteenth floor. That's crucial. They need to investigate the thirteenth floor."

Connor might have a few police under his payroll, but I doubted he had the entire fire department on lockdown. The trucks would roll out. And because of C.J.'s call, they'd have to confirm there was no fire on the thirteenth floor. Which would mean opening the rooms. His whole operation would be exposed. The women inside could be saved, and Connor taken down. Easy. Right?

CONNOR

"Connie! Damn it, Connie, let me out. There's a fucking fire in the building!" The sound of my father's shouting pulled me from a deep slumber. When my eyes opened, it took me a minute to realize where I was. On the floor, leaning against Amanda's cage. The sun had set, and I had no idea what time it was. That's when my dad's voice came again.

"Connie! Let me out. Fire! Fire! Fire! I just heard it on your scanner thing. Trucks are on the way."

"Is there a fire?" Amanda asked beside me.

I groaned. "No. There's no fire. My father is just trying anything he can to get out. Do you hear any alarms?" I yawned as I got up. In mid-stretch, the alarms sounded.

"That fucker. What the hell did he do?" I spat, running to see what my dad had lit on fire to trigger the alarms to try and force my hand to let him out.

Unlocking the door to my unit, my dad tried, and failed, to push past me to get out of the apartment. I shoved him hard until he fell back onto the couch.

"What the fuck have you done?" I hissed.

"I haven't done anything. The power went out, and then your scanner thing." He pointed to the police scanner I kept to monitor situations. "It's saying this building is on fire. The thirteenth floor. That's the one we're on, ain't it?"

My teeth ground together. "The power went out?" I looked around and, sure enough, every one of my non-essential monitors was off. Malcolm. That little shit. There was no fire. It was a scheme to get the authorities on this floor. A way to take me down. Already, sirens were wailing in the distance. There was no time.

"Jesus Christ, Connie. Is there a fucking fire?" my dad yelled. "Let me the fuck out of this place!"

"We're going," I said. "I just need to grab provisions. We're gonna need to go underground. My whole world is about to fucking implode. Fuck!"

Grabbing the three pre-packed emergency bags, I shoved two at my father. "Take these down the stairwell. Do not stop until you reach the ground floor. The doors will be unlocked thanks to the power kill. There will be a car by the dock moving a pet. Get your ass in that car."

"Connie—"

"Don't fucking call me that." I hoisted the other bag over my shoulder. "You get in that car, and you do whatever those men tell you. I'll find you once I have found a safe place to land. Go."

"What about you?" my dad asked.

"I have to do something first."

My dad hesitated a moment, but then he took off toward the exit. I typed quick instructions to Carlos to take my dad to safety. I wasn't about to leave without Amanda though. That's what Malcolm was hoping I'd do.

Marching into her room, I dug out the key to her kennel. The fire alarms were blaring, and my heart was racing as I stared at her cage. I could hear her soft sobs as she waited for me to release her.

It hit me then. I couldn't take her. She was naked. How was I about to walk out of the building, alarms blazing, authorities en route, with a naked woman over my shoulder without anyone noticing? Even if I could make it to the garage, I would have to find a place to hide and shelter both of us. She would slow me down and hurt my chances of a clean escape. I could save her or myself.

"I'm so sorry, Amanda. This wasn't part of the plan."

I took the key, pressed it gently to my lips, then set it on top of her cage. It might have seemed cruel to place the key so close to her while also knowing she could never access it, but old lessons died hard.

My mother had done the same for me. She dangled the key three inches away from my grasp. She thought she was being wicked. But I never saw it that way. I saw the key as hope. Hope that there was a way out. While I couldn't free her myself, I left her the only thing I could. Hope.

Letting loose a sigh, I walked free of her unit but left her door open so the flames would find her faster. The smoke would get her before the flames did, but I needed the evidence of her gone.

There was only one way out for me now. Use my original failsafe. And since the fire department was already on the way...

Inside my unit, I went to the kitchen, pulled out the book of matches, and struck one. As quickly as I could, I set the curtains in each room ablaze, taking extra time to make sure my desk, minus my laptop, which I tucked safely away in my go-bag, were all set on fire. The sprinkler heads would come on soon, and hopefully, the combination of fire and water would destroy as much evidence as possible. Until then, I had to haul ass. My empire had to burn if I was to escape. The irony.

Taking the stairs two at a time, I beelined it down thirteen flights and headed for the garage. The last thing I wanted to do was run smack dab into the fire department.

By now, Carlos and my dad would be on the road. There wasn't time to check. I needed to get to the car and away as fast as humanly possible. I'd need to lay low for probably years, depending on what evidence in the building survived. With any luck, the smoke inhalation would take down Amanda and Belinda before the flames did. If either survived, they wouldn't be permitted to long. I'd have my men inside the police station take care of them before they could testify. What a mess.

Malcolm. I still didn't know how he did it. How could he have tripped the fire alarm without my seeing him? That was a problem for another day. Right now, I needed to get out of the building and get underground until things calmed down. I had more than enough cash and weapons in my bags. I could access offshore funds easily enough. But I couldn't do that from behind prison bars. For now, the priority was hiding.

Even from the garage, I could hear the sirens grow closer.

They'd be here in a matter of minutes. Mercifully, the garage exit was at the back of the building, not the front.

I unlocked the car with my fob and dumped my bag in the trunk. As I reached for the driver's side door, I noticed that the tires had been slit.

"Going somewhere?"

I didn't need to turn around to know who was speaking.

Malcolm.

"I wondered when we'd finally meet," I said, cursing that my only weapons were now in the trunk. Turning slowly, I saw Malcolm in the garage with a cheap pistol in his hands. His eyes were narrowed, and his weapon was pointed straight at my chest. Even if he was a bad shot, if he pulled the trigger, he was likely to hit something.

"It's a shame we didn't meet at my safehouse. If you'd waited just a little longer, you would have discovered where I was hiding," Malcolm said. He took a step closer. The sirens were deafening now.

"A pity." I kept my voice as calm as I could. "Look, I'd love to stay and catch up, but the building we're standing in is currently on fire so..."

Malcolm scoffed. "It's not on fire. I triggered the alarms."

"I know. Which is why I finished the job for you and torched the thirteenth floor." At that Malcolm's body language shifted. "Evidence needs to be buried. I'm sure you understand." I watched him carefully as he seemingly tried to decipher if I was lying or not.

"Where is she?" he shouted.

"Who?"

"Don't play dumb, Connor. You know who. Amanda. Where is she?"

I couldn't help but smile. He'd just shown his cards. He came for the girl. Idiot. No woman was worth dying for. Not even Amanda.

"In her cage. Like a good pet. On the thirteenth floor." I nodded my head above us.

The micro movement in Malcolm's eyes betrayed his emotion. He believed me. As he should.

"Now, the way I see it, you could shoot me..."

"I like that plan." Malcolm raised the gun to my head. From that distance, he'd likely miss. Still...

"But," I interjected, "if you do, then you'd have to figure out what to do with my pesky body without leaving your DNA on me before this place is crawling with authorities. That would take time. Or you could attempt to save Amanda before the fire reaches her. Revenge or love? Decisions, decisions. What will Malcolm Luxx choose?"

CHAPTER TWENTY-FOUR

Malcolm

This wasn't how this was supposed to play out. Connor was meant to come out of the building *with* Amanda. Then I would take Connor down or, at the very least, injure him, and Amanda and I would take off. The authorities would discover Connor's business deals and we'd be free.

But of course, Connor had a backup plan. What I couldn't figure out was if he had legitimately set the place on fire with her still trapped inside. One look at his cold eyes confirmed that he wasn't bluffing. He was sacrificing Amanda to save himself. He was that deplorable of a human.

"Tick-tock, Malcolm. What are you going to do? Kill me or save her?"

One shot. That's all it would take. Less than thirty seconds and I could end the threat of this man. But Connor was also right in that if there was a dead body that would mean cleanup of some kind. There was only one choice I could make.

"This is where it ends, Connor," I said. "Do you understand? You don't come near Amanda or me ever again."

Connor didn't answer. He merely grinned. The bastard had won this battle and he fucking knew it.

Still holding the gun on him, I backed away from him until I reached the stairwell. We held our gaze until that moment, each ready to charge the other if either tried anything.

A deafening blare of a fire truck sounded through the garage, making us both jump. Only then did I lower the gun. Connor may have outmaneuvered me this time, but I wasn't going to sacrifice Amanda for him.

The second I turned away from Connor, I knew that the clock of when we'd meet again would begin. But this time, I'd be ready. I would have time to prepare for his tactics.

Racing up the stairs in the echo chamber of the alarms blaring, I knew there would be little time before the firefighters beat me to the scene. The window of me getting Amanda out of the building without being discovered and called in for questioning was diminishing by the second. Honestly, none of that mattered. All that was important was her safety.

By the time I reached the eleventh floor, I could smell smoke. That fucker. My stomach dropped. He did it. He'd lit the place up. Adrenaline propelled my winded ass up the last two flights, and when I opened the door to the thirteenth floor, my heart sank. Smoke was everywhere. Sprinkler systems had been triggered in some of the rooms, as water was leaching out onto the hallway.

I ripped off my jacket, threw it over my face, and crouched as low as I could to avoid the smoke. I didn't know what room Amanda was in, so I just started yelling and pounding on every door I came to.

Then, ever so softly, I heard her voice through all the alarms. It was coming from the open room at the end.

"Jesus. I'm here, Amanda! Hold on."

Bolting down the hallway, I made my way into the apartment. The lights were off, but the hallway alarm flashed bits of light in a nauseating strobe effect.

"Where are you?" I shouted.

"In here," came her weak voice.

That's when I noticed the metal cage. It had been swallowed

up in the shadows, but now that I was focusing on it, I saw some form of an animal's crate.

It was locked. The key sat right on top of it. What a twisted fuck.

As quickly as I could, I unlocked her cage and pulled her limp, naked body out of it. Tears had dried on her face, and she looked far too pale for my liking.

"Put this over your mouth," I said. I placed my jacket over her torso and mouth. I'm going to get you out of here." Cradling her limp body in my arms, I made my way to the stairs.

I'd only descended two flights when I heard the firefighters coming up the same stairwell. *Fuck.* Without thinking, I opened the door to the eleventh floor and pressed myself against the wall as the rescue crews worked their way up to the higher floors.

Catching my breath in the chaos, I checked on Amanda. Her eyes were closed, but she was breathing.

"Hey, are you hurt?"

"I'm... I'll be okay. Just...hard to breathe. Hurts..." she tried. I needed to get her out of the smoke. And fast. That's when my eyes registered our escape. "I'm going to get us out of here. But Amanda, you have to trust me."

In the years that I owned this building, I had always used the dumbwaiters for more than what the cleaning crews did. They were a discreet way of getting things to and from my hands to the clients. The dumbwaiter didn't travel to the thirteenth floor, however, as that was deemed bad luck back when the designers built it. In fact, the thirteenth floor was never meant to have anything on it. It was technically only there to add to the height of the complex. Which was likely the main reason Connor put his cages on the thirteenth floor. No dumbwaiter meant one less way to escape.

They were hidden on each floor by large paintings. Only the staff knew where they were located. Well, the staff and myself.

Walking over to the painting of a clear Wyeth knockoff, I pulled at the frame to expose the metal box.

"No," she whimpered in my arms. "Not another box."

"It's okay. I'm going with you. It's like a small elevator. It's the only way out of here."

The sound she made caused me physical pain. She didn't want to do this, and I hated that I had to make her.

It took a bit of finagling to get us both inside the small box, and I honestly wasn't sure if they were designed to hold this much weight, but nothing seemed to be giving at the moment.

Slowly, the box moved us downward as Amanda pressed her body against mine. There was no room to move or stretch out, which was probably giving her traumatic flashbacks. I could only hope that my presence was at least making her feel safer.

AMANDA

When I was little, a few years after my mom died, I used to hide inside my toy box. I would move all of the stuffed animals, baby dolls, and blankets that I no longer played with and crawl inside. There was a large plastic lid to the toy box, and I would curl myself into a ball, close the lid, and pretend that I was a bear. I would close my eyes and try so hard to fall into hibernation like we'd learned about in school. Some bears slept for upwards of eight months at a time. I didn't need eight months.

I only wanted to sleep long enough for the summer to be over so that I could have regular school meals again. When the power would work. When I wouldn't have to tiptoe around my dad every waking second. Three months of sleep. That's all. Fast forward through the hell of my life, then wake, rub my eyes, and have it all be over.

That was exactly how I was feeling as Malcolm and I descended. I tried to recall the plastic smell and dust of my toy box. The feel of the warm sun trying to lull me to emotional hibernation... I clung to those memories, trying desperately to disappear. Anything to avoid the burning in my lungs, the ache in every muscle, and the chill against my naked skin. Only the warmth of Malcolm's jacket and his body beneath mine anchored me to the present.

Once the dumbwaiter stopped, my memories turned fuzzy. I remembered shivering so much my teeth hurt. I know I was unstable when Malcolm asked me if I could stand. My muscles were stiff from being in the box, and it felt like I had pins and needles sticking inside my nerves.

At some point, Malcolm made a phone call, and then a vague memory of crawling out of a manhole cover, running down an alley surrounded by the sounds of sirens, and eventually into a black SUV. After that, nothing. Sleep came for me then. Blissful, blissful sleep. I prayed for hibernation. Finally.

When I woke up, I was in a bed. Large arms covered me, pinning me close. My body responded before my brain could, and I jumped.

"What is it? What's wrong?" Malcolm asked urgently in the dark.

My frantic heart eased at hearing his voice. "Nothing. I thought... I thought you were Connor." His arms pulled me closer to him, urging my muscles to relax.

"You're safe now, Amanda. He can't hurt you anymore."

"What happened? How did you get me out of there?" I listened in rapt horror as Malcolm recounted how things played out from when he woke from his roofie to getting me to a secondary safehouse in Florida. His explanation should have left me with a sense of relief, but there was one small detail that Malcolm seemed to gloss over. "Wait. Wait a minute. Are you telling me that Connor is still alive? You didn't kill him?"

I shoved myself free of his arms and sat up. I realized then that I was no longer naked but in a set of Malcolm's clothes. The sweatpants were all twisted around the feet because they were so long, bringing back the memory of being bound. I ripped off the sheets to straighten the fabric.

"It was either kill him or save you," Malcolm said. He sat up beside me. His arms reached out to try and comfort me, but I kicked out of the bed and started to pace the floor.

"You should have killed him! Now we're both going to be hunted. Don't you get it? He's never going to let this go."

"His whole operation was destroyed in the fire, Amanda. I think he's going to have bigger fish to fry."

I shook my head. "No. His Seattle branch is gone. He has others."

"What? How many others?" Malcolm asked.

"I don't know. At least one more in Canada. I overheard him talking about it."

"Well, if he's in Canada, then he's miles away from us."

I glared at him. "You and I both know that will make no difference to Connor."

Malcolm let out a sigh. "I honestly think Connor believes you're dead. That we both died in that fire."

"What? Why would you think that?"

Malcolm got out of bed. He came over to me and held me in his arms as I continued to worry.

"He set the fires on the thirteenth floor, Amanda. He knew you were locked inside a cage. He saved himself and burned the rest."

At that, I perked up. "The others? The other women... Kelli? Did she make it out? Did any of them...?"

Malcolm's eyes pinched closed. My heart sank.

"The only thing I have gotten intel on is that the police scanners reported finding a body in one of the units. Passed of apparent smoke inhalation."

The other girl that was trapped. Death was better than what was in store for her. Still, to die like that.... Only one thing kept me from breaking down into tears. "Kelli must have made it out. She had to have. Or they would have reported a second body. The thugs must have got her in time."

"A solid assumption. But Amanda, if she got out, there is no way of knowing where they took her."

"Right." And there it was. The truth of Kelli's rescue. She might be alive, but to live for what? Being a sex toy for the rest of her life? Sliced and stitched up again for a sadistic surgeon's kicks? Passing in the fire would have been a blessing. "So what happens now?" My voice was dry.

"Now? We stay put. We monitor the situation."

"You mean we hide."

Malcolm let loose a deep sigh as he held me tight. "For now. Until it's safe for us to disappear. I have the resources. We can vanish, Amanda. It can be just the two of us, wherever we want to go. We can start over. New names, new life. He won't find us. We just need to sit tight for a little while. Then we'll be free."

He kissed the top of my head in a gesture that was supposed to make me feel comfortable. Instead, it just filled me with dread. The countdown to when Connor found us again had officially begun.

CHAPTER TWENTY-FIVE

Kelli

"Sit in your chair, Gwen. It's time to go home."

Connor's words lingered in my head as I tried to focus my eyes. I don't know where I am. My last memory was of Connor watching over me in the chair after he'd drugged me. He was waiting for me to lose consciousness. I knew there were two men outside my door ready to take me to my next prison. While I knew I should be terrified by all of it, all I could feel was relief. At least I'd never see Connor again.

But now I didn't know where I was. All I knew was darkness and being cramped inside a small place. My movement was restricted. My eyes struggled to focus in the dark as my bound hands reached around me, trying to assess where I was.

A trunk maybe? No. I was in the wrong position for that, and it was much too small. I can't move my limbs at all. My knees were at my chest, so it had to be something small. Then, I felt movement. Whatever I was trapped inside of was moving. Just then, pinpricks of light entered from some small cracks above me. It hit me. I knew where I was. I was... inside a suitcase.

Opening my mouth to scream, I realized too late that my mouth had been taped shut. My hands were bound with zip ties. Probably my feet too. I debated trying to scream through the tape but wondered if it would be smarter not to let them know the drugs had worn off.

Should I make move when they open the case? Yes. I need to save my strength. Then fight like hell.

"Do you think Connor made it out?" a voice said close to the case.

"Fuck if I know. I wasn't about to wait around."

I listened intently, trying to gather any information that I could.

"Do you think there was really a fire?" the first guy asked.

"I don't know man. But I will tell you this, I saw smoke when we peeled out. If it is on fire, we're all fucked. Now stop asking so many damn questions and get in the car."

"I still don't understand why we need to change cars. What was wrong with the one we were in?"

There was the sound of skin hitting skin like the man asking questions had been slapped.

"One, never question my orders again. And two, Vincent wants this one. He's gonna pay us double."

"Fuck. You're swindling Connor?"

"I'm not. Vincent is. He wanted the other one, but Connor keeps her locked tight. You saw that."

"If he wanted the other chick—"

"Vincent don't know which one is which, man. He asked for Connor's favorite pet. Since that one is about to be barbecued, I'm giving him this one. And if you say a word to him, I'll slit your throat so fast, you won't even have time to scream."

"That's a dangerous game to play with Vincent," the other guy said.

"That's the game we play, homie. Or haven't you figured that shit out yet?"

"You ain't worried about Connor figuring out you botched one of his sales?"

"Connor's gonna have his hands full for a while, ain't he? All these eyes on his business, he's gonna go underground, if he doesn't go up in flames himself. He's not the issue at hand. Time is. Now get her in the trunk. I need to call Vincent. Bring the car to the corner of High and Main. We leave in ten."

I heard footsteps retreating. This might be it. My opportunity to escape. It sounded like we were in a public place. Someone might hear me and help. I had to do something before he put me in the trunk. Throwing my body against the suitcase, I screamed as loud as I could. It didn't come out as much, but it wasn't silent.

"Fuck," the guy said. He worked to keep the case upright while I pushed and shouted for help.

"Be quiet," he hissed. "You'll get us both killed. I'm trying to save you."

Those words gave me pause. Save me?

A second later, the case moved again, but not into the car. It was rolling. Fast. Like the guy must be running. My heart leapt. Maybe he was trying to help?

"Taxi!" I heard him shout. The case came to a stop. His voice came close to the case. "Keep quiet and I promise you, I will get you to safety. But we need to get out of here before Carlos finds out I took you. We'll both be dead then. Got it?"

Knowing the type of people Connor employed, I had no doubt they wouldn't object to killing someone who tried to run. But who the heck was this guy? Could I trust him? I wasn't filled with a lot of options. So I kept my mouth shut as he put the case inside the trunk of the cab.

We drove for what seemed like hours but might have only been minutes. The air was thick and hard to breathe. My limbs ached from being constrained, and my bladder was about to burst.

Just when I thought peeing myself would be inevitable, the cab stopped. A moment later the trunk was opened. And I was once again lifted out of the cab.

We moved forward a few steps as I heard the cab pull away. Beside the case, his voice came again.

"You ok?"

I mumbled a reply, but of course he couldn't hear me.

A second later one of the zippers came loose about two inches. The fresh air felt like ice to my lungs, but I sucked it in.

"We're almost there. Two minutes tops."

I inhaled as much of that fresh air as I could during the next few minutes as he rolled us to another destination. Up several steps, until finally, finally, the case was unzipped.

My body tumbled out and I fell onto a red carpeted floor. For a moment, I couldn't move. All I could do was take great gulps of air before I was able to process where I was.

It looked like an abandoned church. Broken rows of pews lined the back. At the front, a weathered altar stood looming. To the side of that, there was a card table with discarded take-out containers. Some electrical equipment, a banged-up couch, and a folding chair.

My eyes darted up to the guy peering down at me. He looked like a linebacker. Broad shoulders, dark hair cut close, and some sort of tattoo poking out from the top of his dress shirt that was wrinkled and damp with sweat. He wore dark dress pants that were dirty at the knees. While he was intimidating to look at, there was an undeniable softness in his eyes. "Here, let me help you up."

I flinched when he reached out a hand, expecting to be hit.

"I'm not going to hurt you." He took a step back. "Here, let me find something to cut those ties off you."

I struggled to sit up with both my hands and feet bound. I watched with curiosity as the man pushed around some boxes before he pulled out a pocketknife.

He approached me slowly, lifting his hands. "I'm just going to cut off the ties, okay? That's it."

Choosing to trust him, I watched him carefully as his large hands worked to cut through the ties at my feet. I let out a sigh of relief. Then he moved to help me to stand, without cutting my hands free. He ripped the tape off my mouth, and I panted in relief.

"I'm going to leave these ties on for now. We have a lot to talk about, but I need to make sure you don't run. You won't be safe out there."

"I have to pee."

"Oh, right. Sorry. Bathroom's right over here," he said, grabbing my elbow and walking me over to a bathroom in the back of the church. He walked me right to the toilet.

"So, what, are you going to watch me pee too?"

"Yes. I am." My bladder was too angry to object.

I was only wearing a long T-shirt that fell to my knees. No undergarments. That's all the clothing I had been allowed. Connor liked easy access. He used to say my next owner might give me nothing, so I'd better get used to feeling cold. If only that was the worst thing to feel.

Sitting on the cold toilet seat, I closed my eyes and let my bladder release. When I was done, he handed me a wad of toilet paper and at least had the decency to divert his eyes while I wiped.

"Name's Holden," he said when I was finished. "You're Gwen, right?"

"Kelli. Kelli Turner."

"Oh, Carlos said your name was Gwen. Sorry."

"Gwen is the name my new owner gave me. I was starved to look more like his fetish: Gwyneth Paltrow."

"That's fucked up," Holden said and led me back to the couch.

"So, *Holden*. What happens now? You sell me off to yet another perverted fuck?" I asked. "Or are you planning to use me yourself?" I knew it was probably not smart to speak my mind, knowing how guys like this worked, but I was reaching the point that death would be better than this shit.

"I'm not trying to sell you, Kelli. I told you. I'm trying to save you."

I eyed him suspiciously. "Why? What's in it for you? Besides your imminent death when they find out what you did?"

"Why do you think we're hiding?" he laughed.

Running his fingers through his hair, he let loose a slow breath. "I'm not like them, Kelli. I'm a cop."

"What?" I felt the first wave of hope I'd felt in ages. If he was a cop, then maybe this nightmare was over.

Holden started to pace. "I'm in deep cover. Well, I was anyway. Been working as a runner trying to get to their leader, Vincent, but then I got shoved into helping with Connor's ring. A ring we didn't even know about...and fuck. I've fucking blown my cover taking you." He kicked a random empty takeout container across the room.

"If you're a cop, what are we doing here? Why am I still tied up? Why aren't you setting me free? Why haven't you taken me to the station?"

Holden sighed. "Because it's not safe for you. For either one of us to be seen right now. You don't know how deep this goes. How corrupt some of these departments are. These monsters have so many on their payroll. I bring you in, and one of Connor's thugs in my own department catches wind of it, we're both dead. Got it?"

"So what then, we just hide forever?"

"Not forever. Two weeks. I need to be dark for two weeks. Then I can reach out to my FBI contact. They'll be able to move us then. Maybe. If things are quiet. But for the time being, we have to sit. If we step foot out of this building, we become a target."

Two weeks. I needed to stay with a perfect stranger for two weeks. Just when I thought this nightmare was finally over...nope. It was just beginning.

HOLDEN

I fucked up. Like majorly fucked up. Career-ending, life-ending level of fuck up. All because I couldn't stomach another woman being pawned off to a predator. I saw an opportunity to save this woman and I took it. I acted on instinct. But now that I had her at the sanctuary, I had no idea what the fuck to do.

This abandoned church was FBI property. In theory, no one

should bother us. It was a backup spot if we blew our cover. Well, I'd blown it alright. Carlos would have men out looking for us. We were only an hour away from where I'd taken her, and I could only hope that I'd left no trail, but these guys were good. They operated in the shadows. And now I'd just abandoned us here.

"What do we do about food?" I heard Kelli ask. It was a valid question. But one she needn't worry about.

"The sanctuary is well stocked. This place has been operational for a while for agents who are doing their lie-and-wait stints. The floorboards come off. Rations are inside. It's not the best tasting, but it will keep us alive until they can get us out safely."

"That's... Wow. I didn't know the FBI had their shit together enough for something like that."

"It's not their usual protocol, but we knew there was a potential for a shakedown in the near future," I said, finding the hiding spot. I pushed back the ratty carpet and pulled up a floorboard. Inside was a locked case. Punching in the code, I opened the box and took out the pistol. I slipped in one of the magazines and tucked it in the back of my pants.

"Do I get one of those?" Kelli asked. Turning my head, I raised an eyebrow.

"Do you know how to shoot?"

"No. But the other guy might not know that."

I put the lid back on and put the floorboard and carpet back down. "You don't need a gun. You have me. I'll protect you."

"Right. I'm just the damsel in distress. Got it."

I sighed. "Look, I know this isn't an ideal situation. I'm probably going to lose my job for breaking my cover and ruining a years-long operation to save your neck, so can you please just drop the feminism bullshit and let me do my job?"

Her eyes welled, but she didn't cry. She just nodded her head, then placed her bound hands in her lap and stared at the floor. She was submitting to my orders. As she had been trained to do. It made me sick to my stomach thinking about the things she'd been subjected to.

"When was the last time you were given something for your pain?" I asked her, looking at her poorly bandaged finger.

She let out a small hysterical laugh. "I don't even get underwear and you think he's going to give me pain medication?"

"He didn't give you anything for that? Carlos said you nearly lost a finger?"

"I did. Connor cut my finger off with a cigar cutter, then had my new owner, a fucking hand surgeon, put me back together like Frankenstein's monster. The only thing I got was antibiotics to prevent an infection. Can't damage the sex toy. That's where they were taking me when you found me. To the surgeon. He didn't trust Connor to take care of my wound."

"Jesus Christ."

I went to another floorboard to find the oxy we had for injuries, and the bandages, and grabbed a bottle of water. "Here. Take these. When it kicks in, we can change your bandages."

"What is it?"

I showed her the pill bottle. I could see her hesitation.

"That's how he moves us," she said. "He gives us roofies. So, as you can guess, I'm nervous taking pills from a stranger."

"These are just for pain. Though they might make you feel nauseous or sleepy. But hey, it's got to be better than the pain?"

I held out the pill for her to take, but still, she just looked at the pill, undecided. "I've lived with nothing but pain for the last few months... I've forgotten what it feels like to not be hurting."

Her words hit a nerve inside me. The unspeakable things she must have endured at the hands of that monster. Women like her were the reason I joined the force. The predators they faced...they were no match for them. But I was. I had no problem putting a bullet in the middle of the head of anyone who dared step through these doors.

That didn't mean I wasn't uneasy about our situation. She was safe for now, but if Connor was anything like Vincent, either one of them could be on the hunt. One small saving grace was that it did sound like Connor might be doing a bit of hiding as well after hearing those alarms. He'd be laying low. But his goons might not be. We weren't safe. Not even here. Unfortunately, there wasn't anything to do but wait. And pray we weren't found here inside the sanctuary.

***

Thank you for reading! Please add your review because nothing helps an author more and encourages readers to take a chance on a book than a review.

And do you want to know what happens next? Find out in THE SANCTUARY available now. Turn the page for a sneak peek!

You can also sign up for the City Owl Press newsletter to receive notice of all book releases!

SNEAK PEEK OF THE SANCTUARY

It had been weeks of traveling to get as far away from Connor as possible, and I still couldn't get the smell of smoke out of my nose. It lingered everywhere, as though it were embedded in my skin, tattooed on my fingertips, and coated in my hair, despite countless showers. I could never seem to shake the scent.

My bones were weary. Malcolm said it was no wonder with all the travel we'd done, constantly shifting in planes, cars, and taxis. It had been nothing but non-stop movement to avoid detection. Neither one of us had gotten much rest. Yet, what I felt... was restless. Even when we stopped moving, I wouldn't be at peace. I'd forever be looking over my shoulder. I hated that I'd damned Malcolm to that same burden. It wouldn't matter where we went. We'd never be safe.

Not while Connor was alive.

Despite that knowledge, I knew I should be grateful. I was alive. I was out of Connor's cage. And I was with someone who would try his best to keep me safe. I wasn't burned alive like the woman who had been left caged in the fire. Nor was I damned like Kelli, who was likely being used for sick and twisted mutilation fetishes. I got out... but I was still trapped.

Was this how I was going to have to live out my days? Always on the move, forever in disguise, never lingering for long in the outside world?

That wasn't a life. It was a prison sentence.

"We should be landing in twenty minutes," Malcolm said from his seat beside me. He wore a dark baseball hat and glasses with no prescription. His beard was still gone as was the light that used to live in his eyes.

I didn't respond to him. He didn't expect me to. I'd barely spoken since the fire. With so much to process, I was working overtime trying to dodge feeling any of it.

"This is our last flight," Malcolm continued. "Just a short drive, and we'll be at our final destination."

It wouldn't be, though. We'd have to run again, once Connor's thugs caught wind of us. We might have a respite, but there would be no peace. Not while Connor breathed.

"Amanda..." Malcolm tried. He looked as drained as I felt. The dark circles under his eyes rivaled my own. The blond wig I wore for this trip made my scalp itch. I wanted nothing more than to rip it off and chuck it at the teenager popping his gum incessantly in the seat in front of us. But I wasn't stupid. We were flying coach. Private planes would have been too easy to spot. We needed to blend into the scenery. We'd managed to slip under the radar so far. How long could we keep it up?

Malcolm figured Connor would go underground, especially with the authorities investigating what had been happening inside his apartment building. That might have been well and good, but Connor had hired hands. And they would have orders to take down their target, no matter where Connor was.

"I know this has been hard on you." Malcolm ran a hand through his hair. "Once we get you settled, I'll arrange to have a therapist come and—"

At that, I snorted. "A therapist? You think a shrink is going to fix all the twisted shit I've been through?"

"I think it's a start. Therapy is a good tool to use when dealing with huge life events. The woman I spoke to after my mother's passing was—"

I clicked my teeth. "No thanks. I don't want to regurgitate anything from the last few weeks. Okay? I want to forget it all happened."

He shook his head. "Suppressing your trauma isn't healthy."

"Yeah, well reliving it certainly isn't going to be a walk in the park. Drop it. No therapy. If you don't want to deal with this shit, I totally understand. Just leave me at the airport. I'll find a way. I always do." I sighed and pinched my eyes together to hold back the tears threatening to fall.

"I'm not abandoning you, Amanda."

I turned and stared him dead in the eyes. "You should. You should have let me go the first time I tried to run. Now, we're both fucked."

"I would hardly call my situation 'fucked.' I quite enjoy spending time with you, in case you didn't notice." He shot me a tired grin. "Besides, I'm a recluse. I hate most people. I can happily live out my days outside of the real world, if I get to share that time with you. And it won't be forever. Just until the police catch Connor. And they will. They'll find all the evidence of his crimes. They will find him, prosecute him, put him in jail, and throw away the key."

"You think a judicial system Connor has bought and paid for is going to lock him up?" I leaned back against the plane's unforgiving headrest. "You're delusional."

He crossed his arms over his chest. "He hasn't bought everyone out. Having a few local cops wherever he sets up shop is one thing, but to assume he has every jurisdiction in his pocket is highly unlikely."

"Unlikely, but not impossible." I shifted in my seat, giving him my back and signaling the conversation was over. He was trying to dish out hope, claiming a light at the end of the tunnel. But I knew better. At the end of the tunnel, there was just another tunnel. Darker than the one before it.

"Wake up, Amanda. We're here."

I opened my eyes to discover yet another cab interior. I'd lost track of how many we'd been in and out of the last several days. It was dark outside. I couldn't see much of anything. Even so, it felt oddly familiar.

"Where is here?" I asked as I unbuckled my seatbelt. Malcolm didn't answer until the cab had left us on the curb with the two suitcases we'd been living out of.

"My house. Where Connor first tried to sell you to me."

My blood ran cold. "We have been traveling for *days* only to return to the same place we left. Are you insane?"

"The travel was to get him off our scent. Think about it, Amanda. It's the perfect spot. It's the last place he'd think we'd go. No one in their right mind would return to where it began."

"You're not in your right mind, that's for sure," I huffed, searching over my shoulder. This was not a good idea.

Malcolm, sensing my stress, put his hands on my shoulders to steady me. "We'll live on the lower level. No windows there. We'll leave the upper levels as abandoned as they have been. From the outside, it'll look like the property is vacant." He picked up the suitcases. "No one will know we're here. Trust me. Let's get inside before the sun comes up."

I stood my ground. "Malcolm, this is madness. He will be monitoring your place... There could be someone in the bushes right now!"

"There isn't. I have security cameras. There has been no trace of anyone. Besides, Connor's goons will have scattered now that the authorities are sniffing around. Connor is not in a position to be giving orders right now. He will have to go dark. This is the best time to take shelter. And this is my strongest safehouse, Amanda. It's the perfect spot to lay low until he's caught."

"*If* he gets caught," I corrected.

Malcolm frowned. "I know you think this is crazy, but I do know a thing or two about hiding from people you don't want to find you." He dropped one of the suitcases and raised a hand to his chest. "Fellow black-market criminal here, don't forget. I've hidden out in this house dozens of times in my career. It's well stocked for our needs. Now, let's go." He took my hand, and I let him lead me into another cage.

MALCOLM

Coming back to the Seattle house was a huge gamble. The largest gamble of my life. It wasn't the first time Connor had tried to reach me at this address. He'd done it with the video of Kelli's finger and for the picture of Amanda giving Connor head. So, to risk coming back to the place Connor or his thugs had been to multiple times wasn't wise. What I'd told Amanda, however, was true. This was my safest lockdown location. We could live here for months undetected.

But there was another reason I wanted to come back.

In the time we'd been traveling, Darcy informed me of another message arriving on my doorstep. This new message, however, seemed to be from someone named H. Darcy had told me about a cryptic message that was couriered to my house.

It read: *Gwen is safe. Need to talk. Bring A.* It had a street address I didn't know. Of course, I didn't trust a word of it. The message had to be from Connor or one of his men. But to sniff out anything, I needed access to my network. And my best setup was in the Seattle house. Once I discovered more about the message's origin, I'd fill Amanda in. Until then, there was no need to get her upset.

Once Amanda was inside the house, I locked the doors, re-engaged the security system, and directed her straight to the basement. Access to the lower level was via a hidden door on the floor. The couch slid out and the narrow stairway, wide enough for one person, appeared.

"You have stairs under your couch?" she asked.

I grinned. "You don't?"

She rolled her eyes at my bad attempt to lighten the mood, but she made her way down the stairs. I rolled the couch into place over my head, hiding our descent from view. The darkness overtook the small stairwell once the floor was locked into place.

I grabbed my burner cell and flicked on the flashlight. I held it up to a locked door at the bottom of the stairs. To the right of the door was the keypad. I typed in my code as Amanda watched me.

"ALuxx 1005?" She raised a quizzical eyebrow. "What does the 'A' stand for? Let me guess? Middle initial?"

The door unlocked.

I shrugged. "It's no secret I've had a crush on you for decades. You know what they say, manifest what you want. Well, teenage me wanted you. Your name, combined with mine, is part of just about every password I have." I realized how much that said about me.

She looked at me, seemingly unfazed by my ridiculousness. "And the one thousand and five? What's that mean?"

"It's a date. October fifth."

"A date marking what?"

I closed my eyes. "Our wedding day. It's the perfect temperature for an outdoor fall wedding."

"You've been manifesting our wedding day in your passwords?"

"Everyone needs a hobby."

Amanda blinked at me. "I don't know if I should feel flattered or freaked out."

"Probably both is advisable, considering I'm about to lock you in a basement." I regretted the joke as soon as I said it. "Sorry, that was in poor taste."

"But nonetheless true." Amanda walked inside, and the motion sensor lights came on. She glanced around the space. From her expression, I could tell she was picturing a typical American basement: musty scents, surrounded by cement walls and fluorescent lighting. My hideout was anything but a stereotype.

"Are these... hardwood floors? In a basement?" She bent to touch it. "Oh, my God, it's real wood. I thought it must be laminate." Her eyes caught something across the room. "There's a bar? You have a bar? And a fireplace?" She went over to the large black fireplace, which ran the entire width of the living room. Touching the space above the fireplace, she gasped. "That's water. You have a waterfall fireplace?"

"I do. And there is a projection screen that drops from the ceiling for movies." I pointed to the slot just above the fireplace.

"Of course you do." She peered at the large seating area. "Leather couches? Jesus, Malcolm, this ottoman could double as a bed. It's massive."

"That's what she said."

That earned me a throw-pillow to the chest. Worth it.

"How many bedrooms?" she asked, looking around to spot them.

"Just the one, I'm afraid. But if you'd prefer, I could sleep on the ottoman."

"Wise ass." She searched the place a bit more, lifting items and marveling at the opulence.

I'd spent quite a fortune designing it, but if you had to lock yourself away from society for any amount of time, you didn't want to feel like you were in a prison.

When she disappeared into the master bedroom, she shrieked. I ran instantly to her side, fists at the ready, only to see that she'd climbed inside the tub. A huge smile graced her lips.

"You have a claw foot tub!" she squealed. "I have *always* wanted a claw foot tub."

"I know."

She cocked her head. "You know?"

"You told me about your dream house over lunch at school one day. Don't you remember?"

"I did?"

I nodded. "Yes. You said you loved real hardwood flooring and drooled over your neighbor's leather sofas—"

"And that people who owned fireplaces were 'the shit,'" Amanda whispered. "Malcolm, did you design *my* dream house?"

I kicked at the floor sheepishly. "How'd I do?"

The shock of my borderline-obsessive behavior spread across her face. She shifted in the tub so she was kneeling in front of me. "Take your pants off."

"I'm sorry?" I asked, not sure I'd heard her right.

"I'm going to suck you off." She grabbed at my pants.

"Amanda, that's not necessary. I've told you. I'm not going to use you like that."

"No, I'm using you. Malcolm, no man has *ever* listened to what I have wanted. Ever." Her hands slid down my thighs. "You? You built me a fucking living space based on some random conversation we had when we were seventeen. That means something to me. And I want to show you my appreciation."

I put my hands over hers. "Just your being here with me shows me that, Amanda."

"Pants. Off. Now."

As much as I wanted to object to her demand, my cock had heard her order the first time and was already rising to the occasion. We'd have to have another discussion about her feeling the need to repay my help with sexual favors, but that conversation would need to happen later... when my other brain was at the wheel. For now, all I could focus on was her bee-stung lips soon to be wrapped around my dick.

———

Don't stop now. Keep reading with your copy of THE SANCTUARY today!

And don't miss more from Danielle Bannister. Stay up to date on all of her release information, cover reveals, sales, and giveaways by joining her newsletter.

Don't miss the conclusion of *The Captive* series with THE SANCTUARY, available now, and be sure to sign-up to receive all the news and updates from Danielle Bannister.

They thought they were safe... but the danger is only just beginning.

After surviving two harrowing escapes from her captor, Amanda Jackson is done running. But one thing is certain—if she stops now, Connor Brooks, a man who will stop at nothing to claim her as his personal pet, will trap her once and for all.

Malcolm Luxx knows the stakes. With Connor closing in, Amanda's only hope is to vanish into the shadows. But staying hidden won't be easy. With the skills and resources to keep her off the grid, Malcolm will stop at nothing to protect her. But will Amanda agree to hide in a cage of a different kind—a cage built to keep her safe, but at a cost?

Connor Brooks let his guard down, allowing feelings to grow for a pet. Now, he'll do whatever it takes to reclaim what's his—even if it means sacrificing everyone who stands in his way. And with his enemies closing in, he knows one thing for sure: He must get Amanda back—and fast—to cage her for her own protection.

But when Holden and Kelli join the fight, the stakes skyrocket. They've stolen from Connor, and now his ruthless reach will stop at nothing to hunt them down. In a deadly game of cat and mouse, who will survive?

The Sanctuary should be their refuge. But will it be their salvation —or their final resting place?

They thought they'd find safety in The Sanctuary. But the greatest danger may lie within...

ACKNOWLEDGMENTS

As you can imagine, this series is not an easy headspace to live in. It's divisive content, and that makes it hard to know how far to push boundaries and when to back off. To that end, I am grateful to those brave souls who willingly agreed to read the early drafts of this book to help me figure out where those boundaries were. I am eternally grateful to you for reading the early drafts of this story to help bring it to its finish.

Many thanks to Angela Thibodeau Domenichelli and Cassy Bunnell, who read the very first clunky draft of this book to point out the things that desperately needed fixing. Thank you for pointing out the plausibility problems. I needed the reminder!

Also, thanks to City Owl Press for always having the courage to publish the twisted stories my muse comes up with. Many presses wouldn't touch this content with a ten-foot pole. I am grateful to them for believing in storytelling, however it manifests itself. They consistently believe in my writing, even when I don't.

ABOUT THE AUTHOR

DANIELLE BANNISTER lives with her two children in Mid-Coast Maine, along with her precious coffee pot and peppermint mocha creamer. She holds a BA in Theater from the University of Southern Maine and her Masters in Literary Education from the University of Orono.

When she's not on the stage or on the page, you'll find her drinking tea and binge-watching all the Netflix. As one does.

www.daniellebannister.com

facebook.com/BannisterBooks

x.com/dbannisterbooks

instagram.com/daniellebannisterbooks

pinterest.com/bannisterbooks

bookbub.com/authors/danielle-bannister

tiktok.com/@daniellebannisterbooks

ABOUT THE PUBLISHER

City Owl Press is a cutting edge indie publishing company,
bringing the world of romance and speculative fiction to
discerning readers.

Escape Your World. Get Lost in Ours!

www.cityowlpress.com

 facebook.com/YourCityOwlPress

 x.com/cityowlpress

 instagram.com/cityowlbooks

 pinterest.com/cityowlpress